Ras P

There is nothing funny about Putin and his murderous foreign campaigns. For that reason alone, let us laugh at him all the more

Unexpectedly made redundant, Jessica Taylor accepts a surprise job offer selling bespoke sex toys to Putin's underwhelmed harem. She assembles a motley crew of professionals and hangers-on to penetrate Putin's inner-circle, soon finding herself in the middle of a perilous plot to save humanity from World War Three.

Ras Putin – Prince of Russia contains satirical comment, daft slapstick, caricature, cultural references, and silliness.

Dedicated to my long-suffering partner who offered me these sage words on reading the draft of Ras Putin – Prince of Russia:

You do realise Onia, only you will find this funny

Ras Putin – Prince of Russia

Contents

Chapter One 1
Chapter Two 7
Chapter Three 14
Chapter Four 17
Chapter Five 28
Chapter Five 45
Chapter Six 61
Chapter Seven 67
Chapter Eight.. 78
Chapter Nine 89
Chapter Ten.. 100
Chapter Eleven 110
Chapter Twelve 116

Chapter One

The day started much like any June day; warm, sunny, with a gentle breeze. Jessica would never forget the date, 4th May 2022 – because it was her birthday. She stopped in the shadow of *the lipstick*, a block of trendy flats in Portsmouth's Gunwharf Quays development. She smirked and blushed to herself – reminded of her friend, colleague, and previous one-night stand, Onslow Dalliance. For the life of her, she could not think why it reminded her of Onslow – he looked nothing like a lipstick, nor a block of flats.

She was about to move away when a lone individual caught her attention – waving from the penthouse balcony. She waved back to Onslow enthusiastically; now remembering why the flats reminded her of him; he lived there. Her grin wide and reminiscing, she continued her walk to Victory Gate, at the historic Naval Dockyard, and to work.

She had had a tough time recently. Her husband Jason nearly died from virus, she had been made redundant, slept with an older Turkish man, pushed his son/her lover off a cliff and shot a man impersonating a terrorist whilst wearing a fake bomb vest. It was a terrible impersonation – he looked nothing like a terrorist. She decided never to wear a fake bomb vest again.

The second half of the week was no better – she was reemployed as a contractor and kidnapped by Kurdish separatists. She was looking forward to a quiet Friday, catching up on emails and some laundry.

She closed her eyes against the bright spring sun, deeply inhaled the salty, ozone laden sea air, and walked into a lamppost.

'Are you ok, miss?'

'I walked into a lamppost.'

'You can say that again miss!'

'I walked into a lamppost.'

'That is a terrible stammer you have there, miss.'

'Yes. I normally only stammer when stressed.'

Jessica flashed her ID card as the MOD police officer saluted. Two fully armed and fatigued marines nodded. She loves a uniform, recognising the marines as Pitt and Brad from the short time she worked from the Elizabeth class aircraft carrier, HMS Prince of Wales. Feeling her belly tighten, fill with butterflies and flip, she vomited into the gutter.

'Sorry lads. A bad shrimp in my breakfast biryani.'

They moved away from the smell as Jessica continued to a lone figure lent against the fortified dockyard wall in the shade. He was tall, broad, and muscly, with no neck. Slightly older than Jessica, he had classical, simpering good looks. He toyed with his uniform cap, a fixed smirk on his full lips; a man used to breaking hearts.

'Hey.'

'Hey.'

Jessica flashed her ID.

'You don't need that here, miss. Your reputation precedes you.'

Jessica squinted into the distance towards her office.

'I wish it wouldn't keep doing that.'

'How may I assist you, miss?'

'I love a man in uniform.'

She pulled the cap from his fingers and set it on his head.

'Miss?'

'69. Can you give me a 69? I want a 69, please.'

'Sure miss.'

The man now stood upright, his white cap in place, neck prosthetic attached, and marched back into his ice-cream van.

'Is that just a 99 miss? With one flake stuck in the other way?'

Jessica sat opposite her boss, one-time lover, and best friend. Amara wore contact lenses in the office; a security device to stop visitors from reading the reflection of her laptop in her spectacles.

'I love you in glasses, Am. They make you look dead sexy.'

Amara removed her glasses and pinched the bridge of her nose.

'I know Vanilla. But I can't see a bloody thing, wearing them over contacts.'

Jessica loved Amara's pet name for her. Vanilla was the name that Amara gave her when they both realised that Jessica was straight, and that that one brief fling was just that – that one brief fling.

'I'm not sure if this helps, but it reads: *nrecnoc yam ti mohw oT* in your glasses. It looked like a reference letter.'

'Vanilla?'

'Yes.'

'And is that raspberry?'

'Yes. And a scoop of chocolate. I fancied a four-way ...'

Jessica spun around the ice-cream cone to show Amara the chocolate scoop at the rear.

'And?'

'Unfortunately not, Amara. Brad and Pitt were up for it, but the ice-cream seller said he would *get it in the neck from his missus*.' Jessica rolled her eyes. 'As if he should be so lucky.'

'How so?'

'Apparently, he lost his neck in Afghanistan.'

'Special forces?'

'Event catering.'

The women sat in silence for a full minute, reflecting on how a young recruit's life could change so suddenly – in the flash of an exploding hotdog bain-marie.

'Vanilla, sorry, I have some bad news. I must make you redundant.'

'You are joking me Amara! You made me redundant already this week!'

'Really? Are you sure? Bloody Stacy – I swear she is away with the fairies!'

'Yes, she is. Her brother is marrying his boyfriend Roger this weekend. She is bestwoman. Well, you know, the only woman. Norfolk, I think. Or Lesbos. One of those LGBTQ type places.'

'Sorry Jess, if Stacy is away, I don't know how to rescind your notice.'

The women sat in silence for a full minute, further reflecting on how a young recruit's life could change so suddenly – in the flash of an exploding hotdog bain-marie.

'RPG?'

'LPG. Calor Gas, apparently. Faulty valve. Damn Afghanistan, damn it!'

'Yes, they never could make decent gas valves. I have something here for you, Jess.'

Amara slid over a Kingfisher cardboard beer mat with a telephone number scrawled across the picture of a kingfisher. Jessica met her reach halfway, her hand spread over her friend's hand. Amara was of Nigerian heritage and her long fingers made a henna tattoo pattern over the kingfisher.

'Is your palm henna tattoo still wet, Amara?'

'Yes.'

They locked eyes.

'Don't Jess. Don't do that. Staring at me with those big eyes, all gooey faced, won't change my mind. Stacy has locked away the rescinding forms.'

'Gooey? Ah yes, sorry.'

Jessica wiped away the ice-cream from her full, luxurious lips.

'So, what is this?'

'A kingfisher.'

'No – I mean this telephone number.'

'It's a telephone number.'

'Who's telephone number?'

'I cannot say Jess, sorry.'

'Secret?'

'No. I just don't know who's it is. I haven't rung it. But I know you like pictures of kingfishers.'

Jessica tapped her perfectly manicured finger against the beer mat, deep in thought. She wondered how she would explain her redundancy to her husband, Jason. She was still to explain about her involvement with the downing of a Russian jet fighter on the Turkish/Syrian border, and being a murder suspect in the killing of the Canadian High Commissioner to India. *What a week!*

'It doesn't work like that, Jess. You have to tap the number into your phone, not just against the beer mat. Penny Jess? What are you thinking?'

'I don't know, Am. Sometimes I think my life reads like a series of Jessica Taylor thriller novels. No wonder Jason doesn't understand me and the scrapes I get into.'

'How come, Jess?'

'He doesn't read thrillers.'

The women kissed a goodbye. With Jessica's tongue firmly down Amara's throat, the couple fell into a pot-plant and a passionate clench, pulling at each other's clothes - until someone cleared their throat in the open plan office.

Chapter Two

Jessica walked along the seafront, past Onslow's flat, and on to Old Portsmouth. She needed a moment before going home to Jason. She was his *good time* wife, hating taking home her problems.

Jessica had coping mechanisms, which she employed daily to manage her mental health. She kept diaries, wrote lists, compartmentalised, and exercised, especially kickboxing. A shirtless youth, drinking from a can of Stella, shoulder barged Jessica. He spoke with an educated voice – a university accent.

'Sorry, miss. My mistake. I have had some bad news, and I was miles away. Again, I am sorry.'

Jessica smiled sweetly. He was young, far too young for Jessica to show an interest, and pretty. Very pretty.

She delivered her first kick to his solar plexus. As he went down, she repeatedly kicked his sides, bruising his vital organs, but avoiding his face. His pretty face.

'So, *you've* had some bad news, have you son?'

Jessica continued her walk. Jason and Amara both suggested Jessica attend anger management counselling, but with her journal writing, list making, compartmentalising, and exercise, especially kickboxing, she knew she had it covered. She was already feeling better.

The previous month, Jessica and Jason completed a mystery walking tour of Old Portsmouth, with friends. Retracing her steps and calling at each of the Spice Island bars on the walk, she would eventually take a taxi home – *or maybe walk back to Onslow's*. She shook the thought from her head.

Jessica felt drawn to the open door, bathed in sunlight and beneath a swinging sign portraying a kingfisher. Inside was dark, cool, and empty of other customers. A solitary figure stood behind the counter, reading the newspaper.

'What can I get you, love?'

'Kingfisher, please.'

The man slid across a small box, punched full of breathing holes. Jessica heard a faint scratching and flapping from inside.

'Anything else? Bird food? We sell everything small bird/rodent related. We sell a bird wheel if you like? Like a hamster wheel, but kind of inside-out – so your bird can exercise its wings when in a cage. Do you have a birdcage?'

'I have just lost my job and handed back my secure work's iPhone. I don't suppose I could borrow your phone?'

The man slid across his own mobile. Jessica tapped the number on the beer mat. There was no answer.

'Um … try tapping the number into the phone, love.'

The phone answered on the third ring.

'Hi.'

'Hey. I hope you don't mind me calling. I have your phone number.'

'Yes, obviously, I realised that. Who are you?'

The male voice was cool and calm. Neither shaken, nor stirred. A slight hint of an educated Edinburgh accent.

'I lost my job today and was given your number on a Kingfisher beer mat.'

'I remember you at the conference. You are tall and black. Nigerian. Really quite beautiful.'

'Um, not really. I am mixed race, medium height and pretty. Gorgeous rather than beautiful. More white, than anything.'

'Are you sure? Did you used to be black? Anyway, that is an amazing coincidence – we are looking to recruit at the moment.'

'I am sorry, but I don't believe in coincidence.'

'Really? That is an amazing coincidence – neither do I! Why don't you pop in for a chat? Nothing formal.'

'Thank you, that is very kind. I love Indian food, but I am not a fan of chaat. I had shrimp biryani for breakfast. It didn't agree with me.'

'Oh yes, it did! That is also an amazing coincidence actually, but I was thinking more of an informal talk, off the record. Not an official interview.'

'Well, I suppose I have nothing to lose. Where are you?'

'I am working undercover, incognito.'

'Really? That is an amazing coincidence, I am phoning from the Kingfisher Aviary And Small Rodent pet shop – right next door to Incognito's. I will be there in two.'

Jessica entered the nightclub. Women entered free before midnight but had to pay to leave. She scanned the main dancefloor; her gaze settled on a lone figure sat at the bar, working undercover.

'Hey. I am Jess.'

'Good morning. My name is Doctor White. My friends call me Doc. Nice to meet you.'

'Can I ask why you are working undercover, please? Or is it a secret?'

The pair locked eyes. Jessica had won, or when she preferred, lost, every game of strip poker she had ever played – even the one with the Boy Scouts when she was fired as Camp Akela. Doc's eyes were equally cool; cold, even. Both of them – equally even.

'This?' He gestured to the beach towel he was working under. 'The disco lights obscure my laptop screen. May I buy you a drink? May I ask why you were made unemployed today?'

'Yes, and yes.'

The silence stretched for a full five minutes.

'Um, so why were you made unemployed today?'

'Because I lost my job. I was a Project Manager in the international arms industry.'

'Prosthetics? What an amazing coincidence. We are in the same industry.'

'More guns than arms. What position are you recruiting?'

'Ah right, got you. Um, mostly sitting down, but we can stand if you prefer; I don't want you to feel uncomfortable.'

Doc took an item from his manbag, wrapped in a swatch of black rag. He looked around the almost empty bar before sliding it along the counter towards Jessica.

Jessica looked around the almost empty bar before uncovering the object. The barman spoke.

'Same again guys?'

'The young lady and I wish to be alone for a moment.'

'Of course, sir.' The barman walked to the back of Jessica's chair and dragged it, with Jessica still sat, six feet further away from Doc. 'Is that better, sir?'

'What is this, Doc?'

'It does what it says on the tin.'

Jessica read the tin and twist-opened the lid. She took out, and held, the impressive phallus upright from the base. She blushed a little and smiled contemplatively.

'This reminds me of my friend, Onslow – just a one-night stand.'

'Is he well endowed?'

'Not especially, but the night we met, he was wearing a pink latex jacket, ribbed for extra comfort. Position?'

'Some of our customers prefer lying on their front and I know of one who likes to stand. But most lie on their back, apparently.'

'I meant the job you are recruiting.'

'I see. Sales-manager-stroke-project-manager.'

'I would be uncomfortable stroking the project manager. I am married.'

'I meant sales-manager-slash-project-manager.'

'I never say never, but I am not really into the whole golden-showers-kinky stuff.'

'We are looking to increase our markets and are hoping to move into Russia. We are developing a line called *Rasputin*.'

'With a beard and a bullet hole through the head?'

'Not exactly. Look, Jessica, I am not asking you to commit to this…'

'It took me three years to commit to my husband; it is unlikely I could ever commit to a sex toy.'

'… so, keep this demonstration model. Give it a test drive. If you are satisfied, if you feel the love, if you can relate and believe in the product, and you want to come onboard…'

'You have a yacht?'

'… just make contact.'

'Shit!'

'Jessica?'

'Oh my God! Oh my God!'

'I was thinking more that you should take it home for the night.'

'Oh my God! Fuck! FUCK! YES!'

'You accept the position?'

Jessica grabbed the edge of the bar with her free hand, her torso bucking and convulsing.

'I think you had it on the full-spin cycle. We recommend starting on drip-dry and building up. For those who want to save the planet, there is the handwash setting that does not require batteries. Basically, it is a dildo. But it has many computer-controlled settings. It also lights up, plays music, and talks dirty, if you like.'

Jessica retrieved the vibrator and held it to her ear.

'Dido?'

'Basically, yes. But it also has many other computer-controlled settings.'

Chapter Three

Jessica and Jason squeezed an oversized double bath into their small cottage bathroom when they first moved in. It was now their nuptial forum, where they discussed problems, set the world to rights, and washed their hair.

'This bath is too long for this room.'

'I agree Jess.'

'Is that why one end is wedged higher than the other and some of the water runs out over the carpet?'

'Yes.'

'You keep sliding down to my end.'

'Yes.'

'I have been offered a job today, Jace.'

'I thought you had one.'

'I lost it.'

'Again?'

'Don't ask.'

'Ok. What is the new job?'

'Don't ask.'

'Ok.'

The couple sat in silence, their thoughts hanging in the steam between them. Jason not asking.

'That's unusual, look.' Jessica pointed to the thoughts hanging in the steam between them. 'I have been offered a job, marketing dildos to the Russians.'

'That is unusual.'

'Why? Don't Russian women have orgasms?'

Jason shrugged. He was not sure.

'You normally sell arms.'

'True, and they cost an arm and a leg. I think dildos will be more satisfying.'

'How did you hear about the job? Is it a financially sound company? Will you have to travel to Russia?'

Jessica reached for the demonstration vibrator and handed it to Jason.

'Amara gave me a number, which I phoned, and they happened to be recruiting.'

Jason inspected the vibrator.

'Good build quality. But don't you think it smells a bit fishy?'

'I have been testing it quite a bit, but I wiped it.'

'No, I mean Amara knowing a dildo exporter. I don't trust your old lover, Jess.'

'Who? Onslow? He is lovely and totally trustworthy!'

'No! I didn't mean Onslow.'

'Cavus and Albay? I don't trust them either, but they are not involved, I promise. Anyway, Cavus is dead.'

'No, not the Turks.'

'Chris? Richard? Belgie and Netter? The Portsmouth Senior rugby team? Lideri, Sumer …'

'Jess, let me stop you there. I meant Amara. I don't trust Amara.'

'Got you. She didn't introduce us or anything, she just gave me the number. A large construction and engineering company called U-Crane backs the dildo company. I have checked them out.'

'I use U-Crane at work for heavy-crane lifting. They seem ok. Does the job come with a pension?'

'No, I will be an agent for U-Crane, not an employee. But a good hourly rate. It will see me through until Stacy sorts out my job at Company.'

'And you can handle the vibrators?'

'God yes! I mean, a bit of lube…'

'I really meant from a technical and marketing perspective.'

'I have had years of experience selling penetrating hardware that makes the ground move and shudder. I was involved in the army's Rapier missile updates. How difficult can it be?'

'When do you start?'

'Technically, I have already started – familiarising myself with the product. I get paid £69 per hour. That works out at around £92 per orgasm – although I am not sure if I should book for the naps in between. Tomorrow, I have a day of inductions, a tour of the company, meet the bods and agree on a sales strategy. I need an early night.'

'I bet you do. Try not to take your work to bed. Try to relax.'

'I was planning to do both, actually.'

Chapter Four

Jessica considers herself confident and professional, with many years of experience in management. But the first day at a new company is always a little nerve-racking. She woke early to give the new product one final spin, before taking it to the shower, to try out the tumble-dry setting.

'Are you ok love? You look nervous. Are you new here? I don't think I have seen you around.'

Jessica offered the woman a reassuring smile.

'No Mrs Taylor, I have worked here for four years. I am the senior receptionist. You probably haven't seen me before because this is your first day. I am just naturally the nervous-looking type.'

A door slammed. The woman screamed. Jessica went to speak, but the woman continued to scream as she printed Jessica a visitor's ID card. She handed the ID to Jessica, clipped to a lanyard with a tiny set of novelty pink fluffy handcuffs. She continued to scream. Jessica continued to wait.

'Sorry. I am worse in the mornings. If you are happy to walk through, Doctor White will meet you in the open plan office. Good luck Mrs Taylor, he really is a pussycat. Big breaths.'

'Thank you, they are. But they are so firm, I don't need a bra,' Jessica replied, but she was sure she would have remembered if Doc was a pussycat. 'Just not knowing where the loos are and where to find a stapler is unnerving. But I'll be fine, thanks.'

'The restroom is in that corner, Mrs Taylor and, if it helps, take a stapler from the right-hand stationery cupboard.'

She pointed to two cupboard doors at the end of the reception desk.

'Oh yes, I will, thank you. That will make me feel much better, plus I will have the necessary equipment should I need to staple something together.'

Jessica opened the cupboard door as approximately two-hundred vibrators tumbled out onto the floor. Around a third of them switched on, as they hit the ground, and proceeded to buck, gyrate, and spin across the reception floor in all directions. They competed to blast out pop anthems, and Jessica could make out the voice of Jeremy Clarkson shouting obscenities as he chastised a non-existing woman for being a dirty girl.

'The righthand cupboard is stationery, Mrs Taylor. The left is our returns store.'

'I thought they are guaranteed to last a lifetime.'

Jessica collected a spinning blue dildo and studied the worn latex covering, stretched over an impressive gland. Jeremy Clarkson shouted at her to increase the revs, ridiculing her for being more like a Mini Clubman than a Lamborghini.

'That's a fallacy Mrs Taylor.'

'It certainly is phallusy!'

'By that I mean we guarantee them for life, not guaranteed to last for life. We offer replacements.'

Jessica walked through to the office. She heard the receptionist scream as the door slammed.

'Hey Jess! You are twenty-seven minutes late, excellent. On average, our standard-plus model makes white-collar workers thirty-two minutes late for work on a Monday – you are in the ballpark timing. Welcome.'

'Thank you and sorry I am late on my first day. So that was the *standard-plus* model?'

'No, I just explained – you had the *Ballpark*. This way, meet the team.'

*

'Guys, please meet Jessica Taylor.'

The meeting mumbled hellos, nods, and waves. A nerdy looking man in his mid-thirties and wearing a beard, with lederhosen, glanced at his diver's watch. He mumbled *Ballpark* with a slight Scottish brogue – more rural than Doc's accent. It reminded her of Onslow's soft Borders accent. He wore lederhosen.

'Jess – is it ok if we all call you Jess, Jess? We are not as formal as your arms industry.' Doc continued.

'Arms industry Jess-Jess? Fascinating,' Bill the nerd spoke again. He stood and extended his arm into a shake. He removed his beard-lederhosen, folded it, and tucked it into his lederhosen. 'We need to cover facial hair when working in the cleanroom. So, you're an expert in prosthetic arms? The very expertise fully transferrable to our own product range!'

Jessica glanced at Doc. He winked. As her new colleagues warmed to her, she did not have the heart to explain how she worked in military armaments. She would explain later once she had earned their trust and respect. She waved her hand in a balancing motion, demonstrating how she needed to expand on the subject later.

'I hope to bring more to the table than just arms. Thank you all for this opportunity.'

'Specifically, Jess-Jess?'

A stern woman spoke, her hair pulled tight, a bun resting on the very crown of her head. She removed the bun without taking her eyes from Jessica and took a bite. Jessica noted it was a homemade Chelsea bun. *Classy.*

'To start with, I have this stapler.'

Jessica placed the item of stationery on the conference table to nods of approval from the other attendees. Bill spoke again.

'May I see your arm movement again, please, Jess-Jess?'

Jessica crossed her arm in front of her chest and repeated the balancing hand movement for Bill.

'Wow Jess-Jess. That really is amazing; I honestly cannot see the join. And this is actually one of *your* arms?'

'Yes Bill, absolutely. They both are.'

Jessica brought the other arm in front of her chest, demonstrating the motion. Doc spoke.

'Ok guys. Ease back. Let the newbie settle in.' He gestured to an empty seat, which did not respond. Behind sat a young woman. She reminded Jessica of herself, mixed heritage, mostly white, medium height when sitting. She flashed Jessica a warm smile. 'Jess, this is Jess. Jess, Jess.'

The women shook hands.

'I am your PA Jess, Jess-Jess.'

'Nice to meet you, Jess. Please, just Jess, Jess. Not Jess-Jess, Jess. 'Jess', Jess.'

'Understood Jess, 'Jess'. Welcome aboard.'

The meeting settled down again.

'I asked Jess to add an agenda line to this meeting. Did you add Jess, Jess?'

'Yes, sir.' Responded the PA.

'Sorry to put you on-the-spot Jess, I purposely did not ask you to prepare for this; I just want some funky, crazy, off the wall, blue sky thinking, out the box.'

'Ah right.' Jessica blushed.

'Don't worry Jess. There is no wrong answer. Let us just feel your vibes.'

Jessica thought of the Ballpark vibrator stored away in the tin in her bag. She had wondered if they might ask for it back today. Jessica felt reluctant to let them feel her vibes, she hardly knew them. She shifted uneasily on her empty seat.

'I am not sure I am comfortable with that, especially on the first day.'

'Wrong answer, Jess. Expose yourself. We want to taste your vulnerability, think of us as family. What is your first impression of our little company?'

Jessica remembered the hundreds of flaying dildos in reception. She looked around the table of faces, imagining her family – that branch of the family locked away following the unfortunate bull-semen incident.

'Umm. Under performing dildos?'

In unison, the meeting sat back. The stern lady mumbled, 'rude.' A young man added, 'she barely knows us.' Bill mumbled, 'She has a point.' Only Doc sat forward.

'I like your spunk, Jess!'

Jessica squirmed in her seat. She had not managed a second shower.

'Expand.'

Jessica remembered the *auto-expand* setting on her demonstration Ballpark. She cleared her throat, but her reply was mousey.

'It is just that I saw the dildos in reception. The other cupboard. Not the stationery cupboard.'

'Yes Jess, the cupboard on wheels, not the stationary cupboard. The one containing returns.'

'Yes. Well. There are two ways to make more profit. Sell more at the same margin or cut costs.'

'Sexy Jess, sexy.'

'Thank you.' Jessica ran her hand through her bob. 'My husband thinks so. Just thinking aloud, but we need to make the vibrators last longer, less replacement cost. Or manage client's expectations – maybe offer lease options.'

'Yes Jess, make love to me.'

'We should look at expanding markets, perhaps. Untouched client resource.'

'What, like virgins?'

'No.' She remembered her lover Sumer – he was no longer a virgin. Coincidentally, none of her old lovers are virgins. 'Like maybe foreign. Maybe ... Russian?'

'YES!'

The meeting chorused as one. Doc articulated the feeling of the entire room.

'Rasputin, Jess! I knew you would fit right in. You and Rasputin are a perfect fit!'

Jessica relaxed, thinking again about the Ballpark vibrator on *auto-expand* – a perfect fit. She now had them eating from her hand. The young man licked the last peanut and salt from her palm.

'And stop thinking out of the box!'

'Jess?'

'Remember why we are all here Doc. Remember our ethos. Remember our mission, our client satisfaction. Every working minute of every working day, we at U-Crane Dildos should think, live, and breath, inside the box – INSIDE All OUR LADY BOXES!'

The meeting erupted in applause, jumping to their feet, shaking Jessica's hand, and patting her on the back.

The PA walked Jessica to her glass panelled office. The door plaque read *Jess and Jess.*

'Sorry Jess. Can we get this second Jess and and removed please?'

'It is ok Jess. If you look, there is a gap between *Jess and and, and, and and, Jess*, Jess.'

'And?'

'The second Jess is me; we share the office. That is why the second Jess is slightly smaller.'

Jessica looked down at her colleague, slightly, noticing for the first time that she was slightly smaller.

The women busied themselves in the office. Jessica busily prepared for a sales strategy meeting, which was to follow her extensive tour of the facilities. The PA busily prepared her extensive sandwich for lunch. The office phone rang.

'Hello. Jess speaking, may I help?'

'Hi Jess. Jason here. Just checking to see how your first morning went.'

'Really well, Jace. Thank you for asking. The train was late because of the snowdrift, but Doctor White was absolutely cool about it. My colleagues all seemed nice. I have a glass panelled office.'

'I'm pleased for you, Jess, I knew you would settle in. I was just thinking ahead to tonight.'

'Tonight?'

'Date night.'

'Go on.'

Thursday was always date night in the Taylor household.

'Do you want to hear what I have planned for you, Jess?'

She clicked the button to speakerphone, sat back on the chair, and put her feet on her desk. She allowed her fingers to dwell between her legs for a moment as she smoothed her dress.

'Go on.'

'I'd like to start in the bath, massaging your shoulders and down over your breasts. I will rub and tickle you all over until you spin around and take me there and then. But I won't allow you to orgasm. Instead, I will carry you, dripping wet…'

'Dripping wet?'

'… dripping wet to our bed. I will have the video playing of you in the rugby team's changing room on the laptop. I will take you from behind as you watch the video, orgasming 15 separate times, shouting each of the player's names, as you also scream them out on the video.'

'Then Jace, what then?'

'I will flip you over and make love until you shout out my name, loudest.'

'Wow Jace. That is so sexy. A great fantasy. Thank you for sharing it.'

'Fantasy, Jess?'

'I have a boyfriend, Jace. But a lovely thought. Thank you again. And thank you for asking about my first day – I haven't given it much thought over the past 18 months. Is there anything else? Shall I transfer you to your wife?'

Jessica nodded and picked up her receiver.

'Jace. Thanks for calling. Tonight sounds awesome; I'll hold you to it.'

'God, sorry Jess. I thought it was you who answered. Really sorry.'

'Simple mistake to make, don't worry. This morning I thought I was doing my make-up in the restroom mirror, whilst I was actually sat opposite Jess doing hers. Look, I might be late today, but will see you at some point.'

She rung off.

'Jess.'

'Jess?'

'Can we refer to ourselves differently, please? To avoid confusion.'

'Sure.'

'Jess is short for Jessica. I don't mind Jess or Jessica.'

'Sure. My Jess is short for Peter. I don't mind Jess or Peter – you decide, boss.'

'Jess isn't short for Peter, Jess.'

'Please call me Peter, Jess. Yes, it is shorter, by one letter. I use the shorter version Jess, Jess, because Peter sounds more like a boy's name. But I don't mind.'

'Your parents named you Peter?'

'We are all called Peter – my siblings and parents are all Peter. My dad and the boys sometimes shorten it to Pete, whilst mum and us girls shorten it to Jess. But that only causes confusion, so we normally just use Peter. My surname is Piper. We are pepper pickers, but it is quite seasonal work, so I went to college and into a profession. My oldest brother, Peter Piper, still picks a peck of pickled peppers. If Peter Piper picked all the pecks of pickled peppers, there'd be none left for the other Peters to peck the pickled peppers that Peter Piper picked. So, he drives a train now.

'Goodness Peter, that sounds complicated.'

'Not really Jess, try to settle into the rhyme.'

'I'll tell you what Jess, I'll call you Jess and you call me boss or Jessica, Jess. Shall we start this tour of departments, please?'

Chapter Five

They started with the technical workshop. Bill handed the women hairnets and shoe covers for a tour of the cleanroom and development labs.

'Only a percentage of the development projects comes to full fruition. But any, and all, knowledge and understanding is important.'

'It must be expensive if you don't produce any goods following a line of development.'

Bill pointed to a line on the floor to follow, leading to a current development.

'We had a big cash injection when U-Crane Construction purchased the company from Doc and the other private owners. We merged development labs for a while, but then they separated them, again.'

'Why so? That sounds like good commercial planning.'

'There was a straw, which broke the camel's back. It upset a lot of employees from both company divisions. The camel was a therapy pet and loved by everyone – an example of design by committee.'

'What, the straw loading computations?'

'No, the camel. We also went down the wrong path on a project and that cost us, dearly.'

'How so, deary?'

'Half our staff followed the path to Milton Keynes shopping centre, in a round-about way. A serious misappropriation of resource. That is why we now use lines of development painted onto the floor.'

'Yes, the roundabouts are awful, in Milton Keynes. So, you split *development,* again?'

'We also had an incident. In partnership with U-Crane Agriculture, we worked on a project using their automatic lawnmower robot technology. We developed a dildo that would take itself back to a battery charging port when running low. The idea was, as the client slept between orgasms, the dildo would go back to the charger and return to the client fully charged and ready to go.'

'Too complex?'

'No, it worked fine. But we couldn't secure the software properly. We gave away a few prototypes for testing in South America, where clinical trial laws are not so tight. One of our testers had a U-Crane Agriculture robot lawnmower. She was badly injured as she slept – the robot lawnmower ran right over her privates.'

'Awful. Argentinian?'

'A Brazilian by the time it had finished. Thankfully, there was a sergeant who could push the emergency stop before it killed any privates.'

Jessica shook her head.

'We have a law suit outstanding.'

'From the Brazilian army?'

'No, Watford. He just monitors legal things, for us.'

Bill pointed to a suited lawyer through the window, standing out of the cleanroom.

'Is that the Rasputin project?'

Jessica pointed to a hammer and sickle flapping above a door, off the main room.

'No, that is the gardener's shed. Follow this line to the Rasputin project.'

Bill swiped his door security, to let the three into the Rasputin top security department.

'Ow! Why did you swipe me, Bill?'

'Because you were asleep on the job, again. Now open the top security door and let us in.'

'The home workers who test the dildos are often asleep on the job, or just afterwards – you don't swipe them!'

He reached up to the top security door, using a ladder, and let in the party. The bottom security door led to a basement, where security stored various spare security doors, securely. Jessica saw technicians at various workstations and counters, all working on tiny individual metallic vibrators in red, white, or blue.

In one corner stood a solid, heavy looking, steel vessel. A prototype reactor, with heavy bolted doors and a thick viewing sight-glass. Jessica had worked in heavy industry since leaving school, it had often been heavy, industry work, and she had seen similar pieces of hardware. She pointed to the steel cylinder, on heavy steel legs.

'Is that what I think it is, Bill?'

'That really depends, Jess.'

'Depends on what, Bill? Is it a secret?'

'Sorry, I can't tell you, all our secrets are secret. But no, it depends on what you think it is.'

'I think it is a tea urn, Bill.'

'Then it is what you think it is Jess. Would you like a cup? But, before we have hot beverages, jump down off those heavy steel legs, and have a look at the prototype reactor in the corner behind you.'

'Wow Bill! That is the most impressive prototype reactor I have ever seen!'

'Quite a reaction, Jess.'

'Yes, I am impressed.

'We are only running test samples. The female Russian market is enormous. If we manage to penetrate Russian females with our dildos, we will have to build a larger manufacturing reactor.'

'Not cheap Bill. How big is the female Russian market?'

'Our marketing researchers have suggested around 6 feet two inches. Although some are around your height.'

'Wow! That is unbelievably tall Bill; amazing.'

The reactor rumbled in the corner and the outer surface glowed a dull red, before settling back down to a gentle hissing noise.

'That was quite a reaction.'

'I am just surprised Bill. 6 feet two inches is quite tall, especially if the women my height are that tall. I can't help noticing how small the Rasputin vibrators are. Is there not a corelation between height and vaginal size?'

The room hushed. A few workers glanced at Jessica before dropping their gaze and busying themselves with the tasks in hand and also some tasks on the tables, mostly preparing sandwiches for lunch. Bill cleared his throat and pointed to an inspirational poster on the wall above the mess-table.

'Look, please Jess.'

'Oh, my word! That table is a mess!'

'The poster Jess.'

'*Two Legs Bad, Four Legs Good.*'

'The other poster.'

'*Four Legs Bad, Two Legs Good.*'

Bill raised his voice a little, in desperation. His Scottish brogue squeaking a little. He rolled his eyes, a lot.

'Aaaayyee, Jessica aaaayyee, ah knoo. But I meant the main poster.'

'*Madam Twanky Christmas 2022. Support your local pantomime.*'

'The one that says *Rasputin Dildos are the Biggest And Best In The World.* We had better squeeze into my broom-cupboard-of-an-office for a little privacy, ladies.' His brogue squeaked, again, a little.

'Your brogue is squeaking Bill; the lace is undone. Be careful you don't have a bad trip.' She had noticed the foil of ecstasy tabs protruding from his lab coat pocket.

The office was tiny, made worse by the brooms. He apologised, but Jessica just brushed it off. They stood, toe to toe, Jessica could see he had something to say, because he had started to move his lips. There was no space for Peter, so she stood on one of Jessica's feet and one of Bill's, facing the opposite direction; pigeon-toed from an early life picking pickled peppers.

Bill stopped moving his lips, put his hands in Peter's pockets, as it was too cramped to find his own, and let his lips move themselves. After a few minutes of lip movements, he spoke.

'Rasputin is the baby of our regional Eastern European and West Indies Director, Robert Marley.'

'Are you sure? I thought Rasputin was the baby of Efim/Anna Rasputin.'

'You shouldn't swear about Anna Rasputin, Jess. She was the best mum she could be, under very difficult circumstances. Her Efim husband was no help. But no, I mean the Rasputin Dildo Project was the brainchild of our Director, Bob. I am surprised you haven't spoken; you can hardly miss him.'

'Please don't call me Bob, Bill, it is confusing enough with two Jesses. Was he the guy wearing the rasta cap and smoking a spliff on the steps from the carpark, this morning?'

'No, but you can't miss him. He has a large target sewn onto his back.'

'That must have hurt.'

'Under communism, they banned all dildos. Women were to breed workers for the Motherland. And not just the Motherland, but for all the maternity shops across the USSR, and other sectors including manufacturing, mining, and farming. Stalin decreed soviet women should take the labour shortage in hand, by stop taking themselves in hand. Under Stalin, the birth rate increased dramatically and not just under Stalin – but under and on top of all the Russian men that the women could get their hands on. They especially discouraged miners from taking things in hand.'

'Because of their age? Handy.'

'Labour security was a huge priority in soviet Russia. Stalin and the Politburo trusted Russian women to figure it out and…'

'I thought you said they mustn't finger it out…'

'… and meet the population needs.'

'When Vladimir Putin crowned himself Prince of Russia last year, or Ras of Russia as Bob says in his Ethiopian patois, they invited Bob to the ceremony because of his direct lineage to Ras Tafari, or Haile Selassie as we know him. Bob schmoozed the newly crowned Ras Putin and sold him on the idea of mass birth control based on mutual female masturbation for the masses. The Russian's now outsource cheap, unskilled labour to places such as China and Birmingham, so a smaller home population is easier to feed and easier to control.'

'What a wanker!'

'Yes, around 70,713,314 Russian females of wanking age, actually. Bob is not a moneyman, but he calculated that if we sell every woman a U-Crane dildo at a margin of £1 per item, we would be looking at £62,713,314 gross.'

'That is a lot of masturbating – gross! But I completely agree with Bob – he is no moneyman.'

The atmosphere in the office was difficult. Peter fainted due to lack of oxygen.

'But what you say raises more questions than answers, Bill.'

'Queen Victoria and Accrington Stanley. If that helps?'

'How does that help, Bill?'

'It is a couple of answers that you haven't raised questions for. The best I can suggest is you talk to Robert. You should target him, really.'

'They already targeted him, from what I hear.'

'Bullseye Jess. Smart cookie.'

'No thanks, not after the homemade Chelsea bun.'

Bill and Jessica left the broom cupboard in silence, deep in thought. No longer propped between the two, Peter swooned and cracked her head over the reactor.

'She can be like that Jess, always overreacting.'

*

Peter rested for half an hour, before continuing the tour with Jessica. Having visited office and workshop departments, they arrived at the QA/QC office. The department dominated half a floor, right up to the walls. They passed a glass panelled office identical to their own in position, size, and every other detail. Jessica shuddered.

'Boss?'

'It is nothing Peter. Since they accused me of murdering the Canadian High Commissioner to India, last week, I shudder if I see anything that looks out of place. Like a ferryboat disproportionately filling a view, or seeing this office, identical in every way to our own office. It feels like I have lived through this experience before. I know what you are going to say, Peter.'

The women looked at each other knowingly.

'Déjà vu, boss?'

'I knew you were going to say that. Whose office is this?'

'Ours boss. We share the floor with the Quality Department.'

'That explains the name plaque being identical in every way.'

The quality manager appeared from nowhere, making Jessica jump. She recognised him as the young man from the meeting, whom she had had eating from her hand.

'Where did you come from? You made me jump!'

'I came from nowhere, honest.'

He helped Jessica down from the table she had jumped onto and back onto the dominated floor.

As she climbed down, he glanced up her dress.

'Nice beaver.'

'Thank you. But you shouldn't be looking. This reminds me of that scene from the Airplane film.'

'Surely you mean Naked Gun.'

'Don't call me Shirley! No, Airplane. A movie with Leslie Neilsen, but that's not important right now. The *let me* scene. Here, let me!'

She hit him so hard across the face that he flew back into a nearby chair.

'Ah yes, I remember.' He spat a tooth into a tissue and slipped it into a pocket, for later. 'Let me show you around the department first, then you have someone who wants to meet you.'

'My gynaecologist is here? She wants to meet me.'

'No.'

'Yes, she does!'

Jessica handed him a letter from her gynaecologist, asking to meet.

'See?'

'Sorry Jess, you are correct. But this is someone else. You will never guess who.'

Jessica looked blankly at the young man.

'You'll never guess.' He repeated.

Jessica continued to not guess, for another three minutes.

'Anyway. My name is Paul Young.'

'As in Kat Kool and the Kool Cats? Quality.'

'Yes, Quality.'

He returned Jessica's letter.

'Look Jess, I am no gynaecologist, but I'll take a look if you want. I bet it's only a yeast infection.'

He took three visitor hardhats from hooks near the main desk.

'I keep losing my hat. Well, not really losing it, I know where it is. Wherever I leave my hat, that's my home. Probably in the kitchen.'

'Paul Young, wasn't it?'

'Yes, but call me Paul, please.'

'What are the cubicles for?'

'We take a sample of dildos from the production line for quality checks.'

A middle-aged woman came out of one cubicle and dropped a vibrator into the 'passed' basket outside. She stood for a moment; her knees clamped together as if needing to urinate, a hand clutching the front of her skirt into a knot.

'A test driver, Paul?'

'She actually works in the computer room now. But she comes in her breaks, just to keep her hand in. She also has her qualification for doing dry runs, so she comes some Saturday mornings, and bangs out a couple.'

'Dry runs?'

'Yes. Repaired dildos heading back to the client. We use condoms during testing.'

The woman made her way towards the stairs; knees together, hunched over slightly, and using the desk for support. An oriental woman opened a second cubicle door and came out in a billow of cigarette smoke.

'Smoking?'

'Yes, she is pretty.'

'Cigarettes?'

'We have a dispensation from the government. Just us and the beagle test-dogs at British American Tobacco may smoke in a work environment. Most of our ladies need a smoke between orgasms.'

'How you do?' The young oriental woman smiled and bowed to Jessica. Jessica returned the bow. 'I latex intolerant. All material natural, no chemical reaction.'

She wiped the vibrator and handed it to Jessica, to inspect.

'Still rubbery?' Asked Jessica.

'Thank you. I think so. I like colour.'

Paul continued. 'We have a couple of men looking at our new male range, but it is a much smaller market.

'Yes, that has been my experience. Looks to me like a plate of chopped liver!'

'Yes, that is my lunch, would you like some? Here.'

Paul handed Jessica a gentleman's vaginal sex toy.

'It looks like a pig's ear.'

'Yes. We call it our *David Cameron* range. We do a self-lubricating version called an Eton-Mess. The on switch is under the clitoris.'

Jessica switched it on. It lasted forty-five seconds before switching off automatically.

'Damn Jess, you are good. You are a natural – you found the on switch immediately. I'm blowed if I can find it after all these years of fumbling around.'

'Try moving the switch to the rear drainage hole – most men will have no trouble finding that, in my experience.'

'Smart cookie, Jess.'

'No thanks, I had breakfast.'

'It also comes with its own, discrete, carrying bag. Fold it inside out.'

Jessica turned the pig's ear inside-out to reveal a built-in silky bag with no handle.

'A silk purse from a sow's ear. I like it.'

'Also ideal for ladies who like to drink from the furry cup. The ones with hair, tip into a velvet box.'

'So, who wants to meet with me Paul?'

'You will never guess.'

For the second time that day, Jessica didn't guess as Paul ate from her hand, for the second time that day.

'Jessica Taylor, let me introduce…'

'Let me guess. Mr Marley? You are exactly as I imagined. I like the dreadlocks. You remind me of how I like my coffee in the morning.'

'White and weak?'

They both laughed.

'In bed.' She flirted. 'I hear you are related to royalty, Bob.'

'Yes. Through Haile Selassie, all the way back to King Solomon. But you haven't met me to talk about relations, Jess.'

'Relations, Bob?' She giggled. 'What would my husband say?' She giggled, again.

'Um I don't know Jess, what would your husband say?'

'No, I really have *no ideas*. I thought you might know.'

'You have no eyed dears? Fascinating. We used to have a pet camel, but he broke his back. I need to say something very secret, Jess. Nobody must hear.'

She nodded for Peter and Paul to leave. Calling after them she added:

'Come back Peter, come back Paul.'

'Yes Jess?'

'Fly away Peter, fly away Paul. Sorry loves, I always wanted to say that.'

On their own again, Bob continued.

'Nobody must know what I am about to say, Jess. Do you understand?'

'Yes Bob, I think so. Nobody must know what you are about to say. I understand.'

He glanced over Jessica's shoulder towards the open door and the open plan office behind. She nodded, walking to the door and closing it firmly behind her. Bob spoke through the glass panel in the door, as she watched. She could hear nothing he said, especially from where she stood in the noisy open plan office.

He finished speaking and gestured for Jess to re-enter the office. She shrugged, not understanding. He beckoned to her, again. She shrugged, again. He stood up, waving Jessica in. She smiled and waved back. He walked to the door and opened it.

'Jess! I was waving for you to come back in. I have finished saying what nobody must hear.'

'Sorry Bob. You must think me scatty; I didn't understand.'

'YOU,' Bob pointed at Jess, 'COME,' he made walking signs with two fingers, 'HERE.' He brought both palms to his chest.

Jess did as instructed. Bob eased her away from his chest and into a chair.

'Rasputin is at a very delicate stage, Jess. Do you understand?'

'Yes! I'm not stupid.'

'I understand Bill's answers were not of much help.'

'I think I know the question for the Accrington Stanley answer. But Queen Victoria could be the answer to a thousand different questions!'

'We are a team Jess, but I want you to take the lead. Rasputin is my baby, but you are to bring-him-up. Nurture him. So please, ask anything you need to know. There is no such thing as a stupid question at U-Crane Dildos.'

'Are Rasputin dildos tiny, or were they just a long way away?'

'That is a stupid question. Any others?'

'Yes Bob. Right, my second question is: why?'

'Why what?'

'Why are they tiny or so far away?'

Robert looked around the empty office.

'Nobody must know this Jess, understood?'

'Not even me?'

'You can know Jess. You are nobody.'

'Charming.'

'Prince Putin is in denial.'

'I visited the Nile once with an old lover of mine. He was also a salesman.'

'He took you to Egypt, cool. Pyramids?'

'No, conventional selling. Salary plus commission.'

'Was he good?'

'God yes. Best lover I ever had and an expert knowledge of Egyptian ancient history. But never sold to me – I never bought in.'

'Was he trying to sell the good life?'

'No, tractors. Never interested me really.'

'Putin is in denial with his todger.'

'Well obviously. He could hardly leave that back at the Kremlin. My lover certainly made good use of his todger in the Nile – well, in *me* mostly, whilst on the Nile.'

Jessica grinned and blushed – looking misty eyed into middle distance. Robert went to speak, but Jessica held up a hand for silence. Once she had enough silence, she lowered her hand and shook the reminiscences from her head. She continued.

'Neil Parish gave up on selling tractors and became an MP for Tiverton and Honiton. Then he drifted into tractor porn and they fired him. I wonder what he does now. I wonder if he is still a *member.*'

'He sounds like a right member, but who cares?'

Jessica shrugged.

'Sorry Bob, go on. You were saying Putin is in the Nile with his todger.'

'The thing is… tiny.'

'What thing?'

'His thing, his todger, is tiny. He has a micro-penis. Do you see the problem, Jess?'

'Well, I haven't actually seen the problem, but I understand the problem.'

'Smart cookie Jess. Really smart cookie.'

'No thanks Bob. Really no thanks. I had a homemade Chelsea bun earlier.'

'The problem being marketing Jess, as you cleverly worked out.'

'Oh, I see. I thought you meant dates laughing at him. What is the problem with marketing?'

'Prince Putin has only agreed to the relaxing of dildos…'

'They certainly are Bob, especially on a quiet Sunday afternoon.'

'… on the understanding that they are all micro-dildos. The Russian Department of Thoughts is indoctrinating the population to believe that Putin has a big todger and anything bigger is deformed. So U-Crane Rasputin Dildos, the biggest and best in the world, must actually be the size of Putin's micro-penis.'

'But will Russian women go for micro-dildos?'

'I am not a marketing-man, Jess.'

'Nor a moneyman, Bob. Can I ask another stupid question?'

'Better than anyone else I know, Jess.'

'Why are you making the micro-dildos from twice fired depleted uranium?'

'I am not a science-man, Jess. Sorry.'

Jessica realised the meeting was over but batted her eyes at Bob again.

'You are a terrible flirt.'

'Oh, stop it, Bob.'

She licked her lips before biting her bottom lip.

'No, seriously Jess. You are a terrible flirt – that flirt face looks ridiculous.'

Chapter Five

'Jace, I want to put something past you.'

'You can't get anything past me Jess, I'm a pro.'

'I just did: the salt. Do you want pepper?'

Jason spooned butter chicken over two plates of steaming rice.

'What is worrying you?'

'Where to start, Jace?'

The couple stared at the steaming curry. Jason did not want to interrupt her thoughts. Eventually she toyed with a fork full of food and spoke.

'Well for *starters* Jace – African debt, especially now the Chinese are investing.'

'I have done onion bhaji for *starters*. What I really meant is - what do you want to put past me?'

She stared back blankly.

'Just the salt. Anyway, I am arranging a visit to Russia to discuss U-Crane Rasputin Micro-dildos with my contact in the SVR.'

'SVR?'

'KGB.'

'SVR/KGB? TMBA!'

'TMBA? Wtf?'

'TMBA – Too Many Bloody Acronyms! LOL'

'OMG, LOL! SVR: Sluhba Vneshney Razvedki. Also known as KGB: Komitet Gosudarstvennoy Bezopasnosti.'

'I prefer the new name, catchy. A rebrand? What do they do?'

'MI, SS.'

'HWG!'

'SOZ. Military Intelligence and State Security.'

'Blimey!'

'I am thinking of bringing someone new onto the team – well someone *old* I suppose.'

Jessica smiled to herself, blushed, her eyes twinkled, and nipples hardened.

'Your nipples are twinkling, Jess. Who are you thinking of?'

'You Ons. Just you.'

'Thanks love, but my name is Jason.'

'Before I approach my old friend, let me put this past you, Jace. You're an engineer.'

Jason discretely took hold of the salt, for later.

'Well, that's an easy one Jess. Yes, I'm an engineer. Anything else?'

'What do you know about uranium?'

'It is not a material I work with. But I know it is very expensive as they mine it from the planet Uranus, using robots. Similar to kryptonite from the planet Krypton. Do you know it actually rains diamonds on Uranus!'

'My arse, I wish it did! Where did you hear that from?'

'Actually Jess, I read it in a Superman comic, so I know it is true.'

'You remember that much detail from comics you read as a child?'

'This morning, actually. Our engineering library contains all DC and Marvel comics – they are a mine of expert engineering knowledge.'

'My arse!'

'Yeah? I'm up for it if you are Jess. Let's finish supper first.'

'I think we are talking about different things. We are on different planets, again.'

'Like women are from Venus…'

'And you are talking from Uranus! But your answer was actually very helpful, now I know I need to bring Ons onboard. Jace, I need to put something past you.'

Jason glanced down at the salt – it had gone.

'Damn!'

'You really believe I keep nothing from you, no secrets. Don't you?'

'Yes darling. I totally believe and trust in you.'

Jessica snorted into laughter. After several minutes of laughing, she regained control of her breathing, but could not look her husband in the eye.

'Sorry. That is so sweet of you. So, I am going to ask my old colleague to work on this project with me. He is geeky, but dead hot on material technology. There is something fishy about the Rasputin micro-dildos, and I need a second set of eyes.'

'Will U-Crane allow that? They have huge scientific and engineering resource, in house.'

'I might have to bring Ons under the table.'

'And you are putting this past me? Why?'

'It is just Ons and I have history; we will work closely together. He is already on a job, so unless he can do both jobs together, I will have to bring him off first, before I can bring him on to mine. Especially as I won't be able to pay him.'

'Blimey! How well do you know this Ons? How far back do you go?'

'All the way, Jace; all the way until it stopped. We shared digs in Barrow, once.'

Jessica smirked again, blushed and twinkled.

'Ah! I am with you now! Ons as in One-Nightstand-Onslow-Dalliance. Well, if he lets you bring him off and onto your job, it will be great for you to have an old and trusted friend watching your back.'

'Did I tell you about Onslow before? I am surprised.'

'Yes. He gave you a…'

'Yes Jace, I remember. A one-night stand.'

'Any chance he will give you another?'

'Another one-night stand? Well, he is still single, so I guess it is possible. Would you not mind?'

'I am not a jealous guy, Jess. If he wants to give you one, then I say *go for it*.'

'That is so sexy Jace. I love the thought of you giving me permission to have another one-night stand.'

'No problem Jess. I just hope it matches the first one.'

'God Jace yes, so do I! Look, we can heat the butter chicken later. Why don't we nip upstairs.

'Our earlier conversation about Uranus has given you a naughty idea?'

'My arse, Jace!'

'Excellent love, I wasn't thinking of *my arse*!'

The couple giggled together. Jason covered the plates and slipped them into the fridge, as Jessica skipped up the stairs to wait for her husband.

'Where's the lube, Jace?'

'On the nightstand Jess.' Jessica was already in bed, and out of earshot, as Jason continued to talk over his shoulder. 'It was so nice of your old roommate Onslow Dalliance to give you that one nightstand as a leaving present. It will be great if he gives you the matching nightstand for my side of the bed. I think a matching pair may even increase the value.'

*

'Doc, thank you for staying behind.'

'My pleasure Jess. That was a great presentation, well done. I like your idea of boots on the ground.'

Jessica wriggled her bottom on the corner of her desk as she faced Doc until her boots were on the ground. Doc continued.

'But I saw how you kept a couple of things close to your chest.'

'What these? This is my grandma's wedding ring, she said I could have it when she died. The chain is from Jason, for my birthday. I should give the ring back really, nan hasn't died yet.'

'No, I wasn't looking at your jewellery, Jess.'

'What these?'

Jessica squeezed her breasts together until they strained against the buttons of her top.

'Well yes, I was looking at those. But I meant you wanted to talk to me about something outside the meeting. About your Russian trip, perhaps?'

'Robert suggested you are the engineering and materials man. I was just wondering how you got into dildos.'

'My area is really soft materials. Rubber, leather, latex …'

Jessica felt herself flush. She puffed her shirt several times before undoing a button. Doc continued.

'… polymers, natural rubbers, foils, …'

Doc puffed his own open collared shirt and undid a button.

'Thank you for undoing another of my buttons, Doc. I do feel flustered. I can *feel* your passion for soft polymeric substances.'

Doc took a step back, removing a stapler from his pocket.

'Sorry Jess. You probably felt this against your leg. You left it in the conference room on your first day. Robert and I had moved into top-end dog toys. On Christmas eve, I brought a sample home for my golden retriever, Fanny. As a surprise for my wife, Bailey, I wrapped it as a Christmas tree present. I could show

Bailey the fruits of our hard research and development work, and then Fanny could have the first toy produced, to play with. I love fanny.'

'Yes Doc, so I see. But my eyes are up here, please.' Jessica gestured with two fingers to Doc's eyes, then her own. 'But how did you move into rubber, leather, latex, polymers, natural rubbers, foil, sex toys?' Jessica flapped her shirt again before undoing the last button.

'Like all great things Jess, it was by accident.'

'The Hindenburg exploding was by accident. Not much great about that.'

'The thing is, Bailey misunderstood and thought the bendy, self-lubricating, ribbed, squeaky, long chew was *for her*. After Bailey had used it, I gave it to Fanny without realising. Then Bailey reclaimed it from under the cushion and, well, by the time we realised, it was in a loop, all a bit unfortunate. It was still the holidays, but we had to take Bailey to the vet to check for infections, as an emergency case. They gave her jabs.'

'You mean your wife went to the doctors, surely?'

'Yes, the vet's name is Shirley, but no, Bailey needed a kennel cough and hardpad injection. Her GP doesn't offer them. I had her wormed at the same time and the vet threw in some tablets to make her hair shine. Anyway, Bailey growled at Fanny and kept the toy, saying it was her best Christmas present ever – she loved the flapping rabbit ears on the end. The rest is history.'

'So?'
'Jess?'
'Why?'
'Jess?'
'Are?'
'Jess?'

'Doc! Please stop interrupting! So, why are you using processed depleted uranium for the Rasputin micro-dildos?'

'Funny you should ask that, Jess.'

'I am being serious Doc.'

'I know. I still find it funny when a woman says dildo. I realise it is childish. U-Crane Destruction are the demolition branch of U-Crane Construction. They were looking to recycle some depleted uranium, which they had recovered when working on the Porton Down Common Cold research facility.'

'Is that common?'

'No, quite specialist work. U-Crane Destruction was going to land fill an excavation where U-Crane Construction was building a new primary school. Some hoity-toity-namby-pamby-up-your-jacksy-lah-di-dah job's worth, parent of a pupil I think, got it banned on some health and safety gone mad technicality. A real N.I.M.B.Y. Although, in all fairness, it was in her backyard. I thought the playground glowing gently in the dark would be a safety positive! Anyway, U-Crane Destruction let U-Crane Dildos have this solid, very heavy material, at cost price. It is dense and hard wearing. Also, because the dildos are so small,' he looked behind to make sure nobody heard him question the size of *The Biggest and Best Dildos in the world*, 'the extra weight gives the Russians half a chance to find some satisfaction.'

Jessica shuddered. She took her shirt off the back of the chair and put it back on, fastening all the buttons.

'It might satisfy the Russians, but it leaves me cold. Doc, sometime ago, I had a one-night stand …'

'Try to find a matching one, it will dramatically increase the resale value.'

'… and I would like to invite him along for the trip to Russia. I would feel much more confident if I can have my person take-a-look at the science and advise me. He is dead good. An IT and Materials expert. And so hot and good in the sack. He is Scottish, like you, if that helps.'

Doc leant forward, unbuttoned Jessica's shirt and fluffed it; she was looking flustered again.

'U-Crane won't authorise an outsider, Jess. But if you vouch for him…'

'God yes Doc. I mean up against the front door, on the kitchen counter,…'

'Then I suggest you bring him on…' Jess undid a button, '… and I will pay you a double bonus to cover his cost.'

'And the Russian accounts payable and Human Resource won't notice I am a U-Crane double agent?'

'Leave it to me Jess.'

'Don't forget you still have my stapler in your pocket, Doc.'

'No. I am just pleased to see you.'

*

'Onslow darling! Thank you for meeting here at such short notice.'

The couple laughed at the drinks Jessica had bought. An Archers and Lemonade for herself and a bottle of Sol lager with a slice of lime for him – the drinks they would have had when sharing digs together in Barrow.

They hugged, and Onslow kissed her cheek. She lightly brushed his lips with hers, before plunging her tongue deep into his mouth. They stumbled into a pot plant and a passionate clench, before a young woman sitting next to them cleared her throat, in the open plan pub.

'Sorry love. We go way back.'

The young woman smiled. She was quite attractive, tall, and willowy.

'So, Jess, does *perfect in every way husband Jason* know we are here together? Last time you kissed me he threatened to rip my head off!'

'That wasn't just a threat, Ons. Enjoy every day, he will get you, eventually. But strangely, he seems to have given me a hall pass. He said I should let you give me one!'

'Wow, cool.'

'That doesn't mean I want you to! Anyway, down to business, Ons. First, and I am sorry to bring this up, but Jason mentioned the second nightstand. I don't suppose you still have it?'

'To match the one nightstand, I gave you? Have you still got that one? Do you remember why I gave it to you?'

Jessica blushed. She lowered her voice, the adjacent young lady taking more than a passive interest.

'God yes, Ons. I still haven't washed it.'

'Really? Kinky.'

'Not really, I am just not into housework. Although I did dust on top of the kitchen cupboards, once. Do you still use the nightstand?'

'I do Jess. As a knight stand.'

'You still collect Knights? The bronze figurines? That is so sweet.'

She lurched across the table to kiss Onslow again; unnecessarily passionately.

'But to be honest Jess,' he mumbled through Jessica's lips and tongue, 'it doesn't really fit in my posh flat. If Jason wants me to give it to you, I am more than happy to oblige.'

'Secondly, Ons, how available are you?'

'Sorry?'

'I have a job in Russia, and I am looking for your support. It is covert.'

'I would have to ask for leave, from Amara. Although this is an amazing coincidence, Amara gave me a job perk as a bonus. I can take up to three months paid sabbatical to stretch my wings and experience other sectors. So, I am sure she will allow it. What are you into nowadays? I hear you have parted company with Company, partly.'

'Dildos.'

'You always were. I was thinking more professionally speaking.'

'Dildos.'

The couple sat in silence, with their own thoughts. Jessica tried to sit in silence with Onslow's thoughts as well; they probably involved her and dildos. She imagined him spreading his wings for Amara – like an angel. Then she imagined him spreading Jessica's wings, like the devil he is. Onslow also imagined spreading Jessica's wings and then Jessica with dildos. They met across the table in a passionate clench.

Jessica was enjoying her hall pass and wondered how many times could be counted as a second one-night stand. And to how many hours could she stretch the one night. 24 perhaps. Or 48. Or maybe longer if she didn't get dressed.

The willowy young lady threw a glass of water over the couple and with the help of the barman, parted them.

'Do you have to check with a significant other, Ons? There is some danger involved and some travelling, to Russia.'

'Yes, I suppose I should talk to Rebel first, but she is cool.'

'Oh.' Jessica's heart sank. She sat in silence imagining Onslow with clipped wings and her left holding the dildo, alone. She bared a fake smile. 'Rebel?'

'We are dating.'

'Pretty?'

'God yes.'

Jessica kept her smile fixed and nodded.

'Any photos?'

Onslow swiped his phone open.

'This is good; an excellent likeness.'

'Oh my word Ons, she is beautiful. And um …, you know?'

'Fit?'

'Naked.'

'Apart from the stockings, yes.'

Jessica switched her attention back to the photo, using two fingers to zoom in on the detail.

'Wow, even her toes are sexy. Good sucking toes.' She worked her way slowly up the photograph, fully zoomed in. 'Gorgeous legs, really firm calves and thighs. I like the thigh gap.'

The young woman on the adjacent table sidled closer to Jessica to look at the photograph.

'She is a performer. Singer, dancer, actor, that sort of thing. Very fit and lean.'

'Wow! Brazilian!'

'Eastern European. Russian, I think.'

'Pert breasts. I bet she doesn't wear a brassiere!' Jessica tilted the phone to allow the young woman a better look. Jessica, eventually, reached the face. 'Goodness, how pretty? I recognise her, perhaps I have seen her on stage or on the telly. Will I meet her Ons? A formal introduction? Or are you keeping her hidden away from her love rival?'

'Of course, Jess, sorry. How rude of me, what was I thinking? Jessica, this is my girlfriend, Rebel. Rebel, this is my colleague and old friend, Jessica Taylor.'

Jessica shook hands with the young woman from the adjacent table.

'I knew I recognised you! You have sat here all night. I am very pleased to meet you, I know lots about you already.'

'Yes.'

'Goodness. Um, I don't know what to say, Rebel.' The young woman shrugged. 'The, um, kissing, groping, and propositioning of your boyfriend for sex, and all that. Well, sorry.'

The young woman shrugged again.

'Not a problem Jessica. We aren't exclusive yet.'

'Yes, we are, Rebel!' Onslow interjected.

'Are we love? Sorry, you never said. Men eh, Jessica? Are we supposed to be mind readers?'

The women laughed together.

'Well, I can honestly say - I have remained *exclusive*, Rebel!'

'And I can honestly say – well done, Onie.'

There followed an awkward silence. Jessica spoke.

'Um, you have a lovely accent Rebel. Russian and something else. Do you have a little Scottish in you?'

'Yes Jess, whenever Onie can pop around. Normally twice a week. I am actually Crimean, from an ethnic Russian province.'

'Are you working at the moment Rebel, or resting?'

'Working Jessica.'

'Please call me Jess.'

'Ok, thank you. Onie calls me Jess, sometimes.' Another awkward silence followed. 'I am producing, directing, and starring in a feel-good show. Mamma Mia 3. Although strictly speaking, we are not part of the franchise, yet. We are hoping to sell the film rights to Universal Pictures. Judy Craymer and Phyllida Johnson are taking an active interest, already.'

'That is so interesting. What is the storyline? Exactly like Mamma Mia 1 and 2, but with even older has-been actors?'

There followed an awkward silence, eventually broken by Rebel.

'There is a bit of a twist. In my version, the bride is left in tears at the altar, but it is not obvious to the viewer if they are tears of happiness or sadness. We set it in a coastal village to the east of Simerpol, so Black Sea instead of the Mediterranean. We are hoping to break into the Eastern European market, especially Russia.'

'That is an amazing coincidence, Rebel. I am trying to break into the Russian market, myself!'

'I don't believe in coincidence, Jess.'

There followed and awkward silence, but at least they were getting shorter.

'Has it got a name, or just a number?'

'Following *Mamma Mia!* and *Mamma Mia! Here We Go Again*, this third production is called *Cry Mia!* But you are right – it looks like Meryl Streep and Pierce Brosnan will have cameo roles – possibly as ghosts. I am stretched to be honest, Jess. I am also covering marketing and as an agent.'

'You are a Cry Mia! agent Rebel? Goodness, you are working hard.'

'I overheard what you were saying to Onslow, Jess.'

'About my husband saying we could have sex? Yes, sorry about that. Obviously if you go *exclusive*, or whatever … Or perhaps if you want in …?' Jessica tailed off, again.

There followed a very short awkward silence, more of a hesitation.

'I meant about the work trip to Russia. Could I come along, please? I could drop by my family in Crimea and support Onslow in his work, whilst keeping an eye on him and making sure he behaves, with his old flame.'

The women laughed together, awkward silences being a thing of the past.

'It doesn't really work like that, Rebel. The pilot can't just drop you off.'

'I was thinking of tagging along and finding my own way back to my village.'

Chapter Six

Jessica and her PA, Jess, found their way to the director's floor. They looked at the walls.

'Original artwork boss. Very swanky. I would love a job on this floor. Even the PA has a PA! And apparently the cleaner has a PA and a cleaner!'

'Don't be fooled Peter. The corridor isn't paved in gold – stick with me, in sales.'

Doc's PA's PA stood to greet Jess and her PA.

'Doc is expecting you. Nobody else. Just Doc.'

'Ok.'

'So only Doc is expecting you, alone. If you follow the corridor paved in gold, right to the end, my PA will meet you and take you in.'

'Ok.'

At the heavy oak door, stood a PA. She kissed the two women *hello*.

'We are friendly on this floor.' She smiled. 'Please go through.'

'Ok.'

'Jess, Jess! Please take a seat. Just us three, all alone. Or um, you can take a seat each, perhaps? More comfortable, we may be here a while.'

Peter shuffled off Jessica's lap and onto the adjacent seat. They all sat at one end of a long, glass conference table. At the other end was a one-way mirror fixed in the wall, above a drink's cabinet. Three figures stood behind the mirror. They kept in contact with Doc, through a discrete earpiece. Doc continued.

'Drinks ladies? Tea, coffee, cold drink? Whatever you fancy.'

The women looked to each other and shrugged. Jessica took the lead.

'We know you are a busy man, Doc, but have you any Irish Slammers?'

'Absolutely Jess.'

The three did slammers until Jessica felt her nose tingle. Drunk and feeling risqué, Doc suggested the women kiss; they giggled, shaking their heads.

'Doc, may I ask a question before we start, please?'

'Ask away Jessica, there is no such thing as a stupid question.'

'You say that Doc, but is that one-way mirror fitted the correct way around? You realise we can see the people hiding behind it?'

Doc squinted down the room before putting on his spectacles.

'Oh for God's sake! Do I have to do everything myself around here?' Doc shouted, slightly slurred. A canteen assistant knocked and entered with a jar of lemon curd.

'Sorry to bother you sir, but the lid is stuck.'

Doc snatched the jar and opened the lid. The assistant left with the lid lightly refitted.

'I think I must have loosened it for you, sir.' She quipped as she left.

'You may as well come through, people.' Doc slurred at the mirror.

'Shall I do introductions?' Jessica spoke dripping sarcasm, between whiskey hiccups. 'Everyone knows everyone, I think. Except for Peter. Everyone, this is my PA, Peter.'

Peter saluted with a bombed Irish Stout, slamming it down on the table and missing her mouth with the contents. Jessica continued.

'Peter, this is my old boss and onetime lover, Amara, from Company.' She winked at Amara. 'This is Sam Smith, my cross-dressing ex-manager from Company, who took a Military Intelligence position with NATO in mysterious circumstances.' She rolled her eyes. 'And last, but not least, this is Bond, James Bond from MI6. He followed me around Turkey, a few years back.'

They all waved to Peter, who now gently snored from the sofa. They took seats around the table, except for Peter who slept on one sofa, and Sam who sat on the adjacent sofa because of the size of his full, pink ballgown.

'I said I didn't believe in coincidence!' Jessica opened the dialogue. 'Have you deceived me again, Amara?'

'Is your nose alright Vanilla? It is tingling. Look, please understand something, it is not about deceit. It is about who needs to know. Your last project for

Company was selling Type 42 Destroyers to the Indian Navy. Did you run around telling everyone?'

'I didn't realise that was my last project.'

'Exactly! Company is an international arms dealer, Military Intelligence specialises in military intelligence, and NATO is all about a North Atlantic …'

'Yes Am! I get the picture!'

'We all have an interest in delivering a trial box of Rasputin Micro-Dildos to the Kremlin, for Putin's harem.'

'Little-dick has a harem? The poor girls must totally lack job satisfaction!'

'They do. Putin's concubines are at greater statistical risk of suicide than Norwegian lighthouse keepers.'

'So where does a box of dildos come in.'

'Cuming? Well, in the harem dormitories I suppose. But that doesn't matter. What matters is that we make the delivery, and you are the girl to bring it off!'

'What, bring the whole harem off? By myself?'

'No, the delivery.'

'Is there something fishy here, Amara?'

'Not yet, Jess.'

'And U-Crane Dildos' involvement?'

'The UK Government is a big customer of U-Crane Dildos, Jessica.' Doc spoke. 'A sponsor. We received a huge contract for PPE during lockdown and a huge contract for Ferries during Brexit. We received all that public money for doing absolutely nothing, other than me being Boris Johnson's fag at Eaton – now the UK Government is calling in some favours.'

'The UK Government has an interest in delivering a trial pack of dildos to a narcissistic, corrupt, popularist, world leader of low intelligence, with a little dick? I still don't understand why?'

'Yes Jess. We sent Boris a box of *Ballpark* dildos at Christmas to hand out to some of his wives and girlfriends, or Boris Bikes as we call them. How did you know that?'

'No Doc, I mean Vladimir, not Boris!'

The meeting attendees glanced at each other. Amara spoke.

'Um, all it is Jess, you see… Well, what do you think?'

'Is it because you are trying to open more trade deals with Russia following Brexit, improve energy security, and you see dildos as improving relations with a man with a small dick, or something?'

'Absolutely Jess,' Amara gushed. 'Smart cookie!'

'Oh yes, please. It will help to soak up the alcohol.'

The meeting nodded in unison. Jessica continued.

'Why didn't you just say? So, it is imperative I facilitate this delivery and, with Onslow's support, guarantee they are working, and the customer is satisfied. Consider it done.'

'We have a date for you, Jessica.' Amara gestured towards James.

'A date? No, sorry James, I am married. Plus, you really aren't my type.'

James handed over an envelope. Inside, Jessica found a date and time printed on a clean sheet of paper. 9th May 2022 12:00 noon local time.

James spoke. 'You need to have all the Rasputin micro-dildos switch on at this exact time.'

'But that is only four days away. Why?'

'It's a surprise.'

'Oh great! I love a surprise.'

'Not a surprise for you, Jess. A surprise for Putin.'

'Go on.'

The three looked at each other and shrugged. They looked at Doc, who also shrugged. The four looked at each other and they all shrugged. Sam spoke.

'Well, we programmed them to sing *Happy Victory Day Parade* in Russian.'

'Is that even a song? I have never heard it. Look, I need to get a move on, I haven't much time.'

Jessica pulled a sleeping PA onto her back and piggybacked her to their floor.

Chapter Seven

'This is your captain, speaking. Welcome aboard this private flight from Heathrow...' The passengers heard a muffled conversation between the captain and co-pilot, looking at a map stretched across their laps. The co-pilot nodded, and the captain continued, *'... London. We will land in Moscow ...'* there followed more mumbling as the co-pilot flicked through a Moscow AtoZ before nodding again *'... Russia. We hope to land at 0800 hours local time...'* more mumbling *'... which might be local to Heathrow or Moscow, we are not quite sure, but definitely no later than 8 am. Everything is different because we cannot fly over Ukraine at the moment.'*

Jessica sat in the front row, next to the sleeping navigator and directly behind the captain.

'Sorry to interrupt Captain Speaking, but you don't need to speak through the intercom, we can hear you perfectly well without.'

The co-pilot was a middle-aged woman, with a friendly, open smile. The captain was tall, handsome, with a full beard. Jessica continued.

'And if we can't fly over Ukraine, what will we do? Taxi along the motorway?'

'Please Mrs Taylor, call me Barbara.' She smiled through her beard. 'That was my question exactly! I was all for giving it a go, but your cabin manager for the flight, Sharon, had a look on the Uber App and has found a shorter route. I pressed the *pay now* button by mistake – but air traffic control is trying to cancel the taxi without losing Uber user points.'

Sharon started the safety instructions and inadvertently inflated her life jacket. Flaying around like a Michelin Man, wearing a little too much foundation in the limited space of the Learjet, she fell backwards into the toilet, waking the navigator. He shouted *kinky* and dived in after her, slamming shut the door. The pilot mumbled into the intercom.

'We need to have a word with those two!'

The co-pilot nodded.

Onslow took his seat next to Jessica. He was terrified of flying and began his routine of rubbing sweaty palms over his thighs. At least this time, he kept his trousers on. Jessica gripped his arm for comfort and tried to distract him with small talk.

'I've had my hair cut short; do you like it?'

'Yeah.'

'I had it in a bob over winter. But my PA, Jess, had the same bob, so I decided it was time for a change.'

Onslow glanced at Peter, sat in the row behind, and back to Jessica.

'But she has the same haircut as you, now. Really short, like Betty Boop.'

'I know. What an amazing coincidence. She had her hair cut like Betty Boop this morning, to look different from me!'

'I am not really a believer, Jess.'

'In coincidence? No, me neither.'

'No. I don't believe in Betty Boop; she is only a cartoon character.'

The jet roared along the runway and took to the sky as Onslow clenched Jessica's fingers, cracking her knuckles. Jessica continued to distract him.

'I will have my hair done again next week. I will have it cut longer, this time.'

Onslow relaxed, sweat running over his neck.

'Yeah. Whatever.' He took a deep breath, glancing at his watch. 'How much longer?'

'Probably down my back; right down to my bum.'

'Thanks for distracting me, Jess. I hate flying.'

Rebel spoke from her seat next to Peter.

'Ok Jessica. You may let go of my boyfriend's hand now! Unless you had planned to take him into the mile high club?'

'Sorry Rebel.' She released his hand. 'Honestly, I was not planning on having sex with him in the loo.'

There was an awkward silence, reminding both women of the old days. Jessica continued, attempting to engage her love rival.

'You see, Jason only gave me a hall pass for a second night stand. I don't want to waste it on a quickie in the loo. Can you give me some notice before you two go exclusive, Rebel, please?'

Rebel appreciated Jessica trusting and confiding in her - regarding Jessica's intention to seduce her boyfriend.

'Yes Jessica, of course. There is a time difference in your favour when flying home. He could start rogering you in Moscow, continue on the plane, and you'll have an extra two hours before the second night ends.'

'You are a gem, Rebel, good call. I am so pleased you came on the trip. Onslow, have you checked our cargo? What is your view on the materials used and the information technology employed?'

'I like the individual tins they come in. Quaint.'

'Yes, a branding thing, but obviously the client needs to take them out, to come. My Ballpark vibrator came in a can. A unique selling point.'

'More than that Jess. These cans are lead. The Rasputin micro-dildos are depleted uranium. If they were not protected inside individual lead cans, they would form a critical mass in close proximity, and there would be a nuclear explosion.'

'What!'

'Take your headphones off, Jess! These cans are lead. The Rasputin micro-dildos are made from depleted uranium. If they are not protected inside individual lead cans, they would form a critical mass when in close proximity, and there would be a nuclear reaction and explosion; a dirty, dirty bomb.'

Jessica imagined this last phrase spoken by Jeremy Clarkson, for some reason.

'How big an explosion?'

'Well, enough to blow this aircraft out the sky.'

The flight attendant screamed. Jessica turned to Rebel.

'I think they have finished if you and Onslow want to use the loo next.'

'No Jess, this is interesting. Carry-on Onie.'

'Dirty bombs are notoriously difficult to predict. But if all or most dildos were within, say, three yards of each other, forming a critical mass, they may spontaneously chain-react, causing a nuclear explosion. If one or more of the dildos are stimulated, then that might start the reaction. If, say, all the dildos are carefully unpacked, within a three-yard radius, and detonated in a controlled way, then the explosion would be quite substantial.'

The flight attendant screamed again.

'Actually Rebel, you were right to hang back. I think they are still at it. Stimulated?'

'If an electric current, mechanical impact, vigorous rubbing, or even a sudden acoustic shock excites the unstable molecules and atoms, it will release neutrons from the uranium atoms. Each released neutron would cause further fission, further releases, and in the blink of an eye, you have a nuclear explosion.'

'Wow. But the lead cans will contain an explosion?'

'Absolutely not Jess. The lead cans prevent the critical mass forming, initially. Once the reaction starts, everything around the intense energy release will vaporise – air, concrete, lead, everything. This adds 'fuel' to the explosion. There are computer chips to control the fission, we call them fission chips, but they are inherently unstable.'

'Onslow, are you in any way surprised that they made the dildos of depleted uranium? Is it an obvious choice of engineering material to select for domestic use?'

Rebel spoke. 'Jess, I am going to stop you there. Onie, the loo is empty now. Shall we join the club?'

The couple left for the loo. Jessica felt a little surprised they were not concentrating on the unfolding situation, but she knew how difficult Onslow was to resist. She then remembered the naked photo of Rebel and those sexy sucking toes. She sighed and sat back. Peter spoke.

'Boss. I think you need to face facts.'

'Yes Peter, you are right. We need to visit the hairdresser together next time, to avoid confusion.'

'I was also thinking we need to think about our actual mission here, boss.'

'Are you thinking what I am thinking, Peter?'

'Yes boss. If you think we are on a mission to decapitate the Russian regime and nuke half of the weaponry in the Victory Parade, then we are thinking the same thing.'

'Actually, I was thinking we should dye our hair, but different colours.'

'That is an amazing coincidence, boss. I thought that, as well as us sabotaging a world nuclear power.'

The couple returned from the toilet, wiping their hands and panting.

'Sorry, we were as quick as possible.'

'Slightly smaller Jess, and I, think they have sent us on a secret mission to nuke Putin and the Victory Parade. Onslow love, you have nail varnish around your mouth.'

'Actually Jess, I was going to suggest we turn around and fly home.'

Onslow lowered his voice, so only those in his group could hear. Captain Speaking moved back from the pilot's seat and squeezed into the non-existent gap between Rebel and Peter.

'Sorry guys. I couldn't hear what you were saying from outside your group.'

Onslow lowered his voice again and repeated his thoughts for the captain's benefit.

'Ah, that's better. The thing is, I am under strict instructions to take you to Moscow,...' She mumbled into her head-mic and pressed her finger against her earpiece to hear her navigator's reply. '... Russia. I will not turn around.'

She turned around so Rebel and Peter could hear. Rebel now spoke.

'Jess, I love my work with the production company. But I am not just a Cry Mia! agent. It is also a cover, so no one suspects I am a Crimea agent.'

The flight attendant shouted *'I knew it! I said she was!'* The navigator added *'You did. Well done!'* They huddled around the navigator's headphones, listening to the top-secret conversation through Barbara Speaking's speaking-microphone. Rebel continued.

'I love my work, but there are dangers.'

'What sort of dangers, Rebel?' Asked Onslow.

'We had a dancer break an ankle, and last week a singer broke her voice. But I was going to say, my mission, should I accept it, is to support you guys to deliver the dildos and have them stimulated. Then to try to get you out before the big bangs start.'

'So, am I just part of your cover, Rebel?'

'No Onie! That was a complete coincidence, honest. I really love you.'

Jessica and Rebel made eye contact and both women burst out laughing. Jessica turned to Peter.

'And your role in this, Jess Piper?'

'To take minutes.'

'You have taken none for this meeting.'

'Shit boss, sorry. I clean forgot.'

*

The five sat in the dimmed lighting of the aircraft cabin, each with their own thoughts. Onslow's and Jessica's thoughts were quite similar, and both involved Rebel's toes. Despite Barbara having forced herself into the non-existent gap between Peter and Rebel, the three managed some sleep until the flight attendant, Sharon, woke them, rattling the duty-free trolley down the aisle.

'Captain Speaking, sorry to trouble you, but we can see the runway.'

'Shit! Why didn't you wake me earlier?'

'The co-pilot didn't want to disturb you; you looked so peaceful. But she did say to also let you know – we ran out of fuel some time ago.'

'Double shit! We were supposed to refuel in Poland. Fuel is cheap there, and I was going to use my Selgros loyalty card!'

Barbara clambered over Rebel and slowly made her way to the cockpit behind Sharon, as she finished selling duty-free goods and manoeuvred the trolley into the galley.

The Learjet hit the grass area short of the runway, bounced and landed on the runway apron. In a cloud of dust and burnt rubber, the aircraft came to a halt, at a third of the way towards the terminal building. The crew clapped. The captain radioed the flight tower.

'Moscow Moscow. Private aircraft U-Crane 69. Touched down. Over.'

'U-Crane 69, received. Are we expecting you? Over.'

'Sorry I didn't call ahead. We had a few problems. We didn't stop for fuel, so are ahead of schedule. Permission to taxi over. Over.'

'Roger.'

'Barbara here, Moscow. Roger is in Norfolk marrying his boyfriend. Over.'

'Roger Barbara. Ova here, please give Roger my love, Over.'

'Over there? Over.'

'Ova, Barbara, Ova. Roger Barbara?'

'Roger Ova. Copy.'

'Ok: Roger Ova. Was that ok, Barbara? Roger? Over.'

'Roger is in … Look, Ova, …'

'Look at what? Over.'

'Break! You interrupted me Ova …'

'Sorry Barbara. Over.'

'Break! You did it again, Ova! Don't you speak until I say *over*, Ova. Over.'

'Roger Barbara. Barbara, the airport is shut, I am the cleaner, Ova. But I am sure you can taxi over. Over.'

'Ova, you must stop saying over in the middle of a sentence. It is confusing. Over.'

'It doesn't confuse me.'

There followed a silence.

'Over?'

'What?'

'Ova…'

'What?'

'… we are out of fuel. May I call a taxi over, Ova? Over.'

'Roger Barbara. Can't see why not. Call a taxi over. Over.'

'Ova, can you call a local taxi please? Uber has suspended my account over an earlier misunderstanding. Over.'

'Wilco, roger? Over.'

'Wilco what, Ova? Over.'

'Wilco is my cousin. He has a taxi and a fish canning factory. Over.'

'Fish factory, Ova? Is that relevant or just a red herring? Over.'

'Salted herring. Salted over…'

'Ova, …'

'Break! I haven't finished Barbara. Salted herring over rye is best. I'll ask Wilco to bring you some. You stay there Barbara. Wilco is on his way. He's also bringing a tow rope and a can of fuel.'

'Wilco roger, Ova. Over and out.'

The passengers clapped, whooped, and hugged each other.

Chapter Eight

The taxi journey to the Kremlin was very short, so short that they had to get the bus for the remainder. The box of dildos was very heavy. Jessica spoke to Wilco, the taxi driver.

'You cannot blame us for this Wilco. We asked you to take us to the Kremlin. Not the Kremlin Herring and Kebab Takeaway! I need you to take us four paying customers to the actual Kremlin.'

'I am sorry missus. I don't like to drive in the city centre. All those cars.'

'How much do I have to pay to take us and the box to the Kremlin? The actual Kremlin, with no backing out, this time.'

Wilco pondered the situation for a full minute.

'Ok. I am an honourable Russian fish canner. 10,000 Ruble to take you. The box goes free.'

'Deal.' They shook hands. 'You take the box for free; we'll catch the bus. See you there.'

Heavily armed security whisked them through the outer gates and the inner gates towards the outer porch and into the inner porch,. One had such heavy arms that he reminded Jessica of an orangutan. A heavily armed butler met them in the outer hall and took them to the inner hall. A member of Putin's personal bodyguard took them through the inner hall to the outer sanctum. At one point they found themselves on the street by mistake and had to start again.

'What is your business here?' barked another orangutan in a suit that did not suit. His arms were not heavy, but he was orange with bright yellow hair. He had tiny monkey hands, compared to the rest of his bloated body. He had an American accent. Jessica recognised him. She whispered to Peter.

'If that is who I think it is, it will trump all the other stories we take home with us.'

Peter took minutes. Jessica whispered louder.

'In a minute Peter! Not yet.'

The orangutan barked again.

'You are a beautiful piece of ass – but nobody sees the boss without getting past me first.'

He extended a tiny monkey hand to shake. Jessica recoiled. Another suit appeared, which suited the person inside. He shooed at the orangutan in the suit.

'Donald, off you go. We will get you out for the 2024 *presidentials*. Now shoo! Sorry about that. We spoil him and it shows. The boss is the worst – he even lets him eat at the table.' The suit grimaced and laughed. 'Vodka?'

The party sat around the desk and accepted several rounds of vodka. Jessica had done her social etiquette homework and knew how the Russians did business. Peter started singing rugby songs.

'Sorry. I can't take her anywhere.'

'No? You took her here.'

'Good point. We are here on a delicate matter. Your boss is expecting us.'

'Indeed, Mrs Taylor. In the box?'

'Yes.'

'All 24 in that,' the suit studied the tiny box from his seat, 'massive box?'

'Yes. And it weighs a ton.'

The suit smiled and winked.

'No seriously. It weighs a ton.'

'Oh, is that normal?'

'We specially manufactured them to your agreed specification. This sample is a gift to Prince Putin and his overworked harem. To help them... relax after a busy day. There are no strings attached.'

'Really? No strings? Isn't there a chance they might, you know, slip right inside?'

'This may eventually lead to a larger...'

'Larger? Impossible!' The suit looked around for eavesdroppers.

'... supply, should you wish to distribute to the wider population.'

'The wider population? Wouldn't they be more suited to the narrower population?'

'What do all the little Russian women do, while you big men are playing with your guns on Victory Parade Day?'

'Some are down the mines, in the factories, flying jet fighters, steering ...'

Jessica changed tack.

'It's just that I imagine the harem would fiddle around all day, waiting for their *man*. We know how busy Prince Putin must be on parade day, so I was wondering if the ladies should unpack the dildos on the day, carefully. Say noon on 9th May. All turn them on at the same time and enjoy the arousing music that we have set them to play.'

'*Rousing* music?'

'That is what I said.'

'I tend not to dip into the harem, Mrs Taylor. But I could put forward your suggestion.'

'My understanding is that we would have a brief audience with the main man. I would like to present the idea myself, if possible.'

She leant forward and batted her eyes. He leant forward and batted his back. He slid his hand onto the table. She had done her homework – no such thing as *something for nothing*. She slid her hand into her bag and slid the stapler across the table. He leant back, stopped batting, opened a desk drawer, and slid in his bribe. They drank more vodka. Peter passed out.

'Nice office you have here.' She flattered.

'Yes, the Kremlin used to be a citadel built mostly in the fifteenth century, with some parts dating back to the twelfth century.'

'Really? Goodness, some history. What is it now?'

'Now it is a citadel built mostly in the fifteenth century, with some parts dating back to the twelfth century. Mrs Taylor, I am just a pussycat…'

'Oh! I thought that was the vodka.'

'… but the boss is no fool. I hope you can perform under pressure.'

'Damn, I should have done more homework. I know all the words to Bohemian Rhapsody if he can hum the tune.'

They were taken from the outer sanctum to the inner sanctum. Onslow whispered to Jessica.

'Have you noticed how the rooms get smaller? Not just subsequent rooms, but each individual room.'

'Yes Ons. It is like something from Alice Through the Looking Glass.'

'Please wait here. The boss will arrive soon.' Offered the assistant.

The four stood in an awkward silence. Peter and Onslow now empathising with Jessica and Rebel, with their history of awkward silences.

'Rebel,' started Jessica, 'I am unhappy about this. We could kill innocent members of the public.'

'Innocent people? Who, Russians?'

'Rebel!' All three shouted at Rebel, together.

'What?'

Onslow continued.

'That is a bit racist, Rebel. Of course, some Russians can be innocent!'

'Grow some balls you lot! Political correctness gone mad! They started it!'

'How do you make that out, Rebel?'

'They invaded Ukraine!'

The awkward silence became more awkward.

'And what about the harem, Rebel?' Offered Onslow.

Peter intervened.

'Look guys. We have to accept there will be collateral damage. Crimea, and Ukraine, are being annexed by Russia. We need to defeat them.'

'I thought Volodymyr was winning the war against the Russians single-handed!' All four pondered Onslow's observation. 'He is such a hunk, but so vulnerable. I have never had such a celebrity crush before. I'd have his babies.'

All three now pondered Onslow's unexpected declaration of love for the Ukraine president.

The awkward silence continued, but with some metro-male-liberal enlightenment.

Jessica spoke.

'He is winning the war, but at enormous cost and losses. This one act could end the madness. Losing 24 sex workers…'

'Jess!' All three shouted together.

'What?'

Peter retorted. 'Fucking hell boss! Talk about scratch the liberal to smell the fascist underneath!'

There was no time for any silences.

'Peter!' All three shouted together.

'What?'

'You can't go around accusing Jessica of being a fascist!'

'Whatever. How come we haven't shouted at Onslow?'

A ponderous silence followed.

All three pondered Onslow's unexpected declaration of love for the Ukraine president.

'Yes, it is strange how everything Onslow does is sexy, endearing, or both.' suggested Jessica.

The door at the opposite end of the room opened and a topless Putin rode in on the back of a thoroughbred stallion. He rode closer to the group, looking at them, up his nose.

'That's odd, Onslow,' Jessica whispered, 'how come he is on the back of a horse, but looking up at us?'

'So? How may you help me?' The president's voice was high and squeaky. The four had only previously heard his words spoken through the dulcet toned interpreter on television news. They all burst into fits of giggles.

'Excuse me? You have come from the west, bearing gifts. I have been expecting you.'

He extended his arm towards Jessica. She accepted his limp wristed, wet fish handshake.

'Herring? Thank you.'

'Smart cookie, Mrs Taylor.'

'No, thank you. This salted herring will be fine. Please call me Jess.'

He leant up and kissed her hand. She felt a little vertigo. He rode his horse behind a large wooden desk and dismounted. Jessica took a step forward and bumped her head on the ceiling.

'Ons? What the fuck?' She whispered.

'The room is slanting away from us, like the trick rooms at the fairground. My guess is, it is to make the president look taller than he really is.'

The assistant, who had accepted the stapler as a bribe, entered the room, picked up the horse, put it under his arm, and left.

'So? You have brought me 24 extra heavy duty, amazingly huge, dildos for the ladies in my harem?'

Peter sniggered, the vodka still influencing her decision making.

The president ordered more vodka for the group. He seemingly held a pint glass. Jessica glanced at Onslow, who discretely shook his head.

'Yes Ras.' Jessica answered. 'And, if you like them, we can supply enough to meet your national birth control needs. But one step at a time.'

More vodka poured.

'Are these dildos good?'

'I have not personally tried this model. It is bespoke and unique to yourselves. But I can vouch for U-Crane Dildos, generally. Especially the *Ballpark*.'

'Mrs Taylor, I wonder…'

'I mean honestly Vlad; may I call you Vlad? I couldn't get enough of it!'

'Yes, Vlad is fine. I am…'

'It had me in the shower, at the traffic lights, on the phone to mother. It is really quite addictive.'

'I...'

'First thing in the morning, in the loos at work. I can see why some housewives report they must bury them in the garden, so they can get on with childcare. I mean...'

Onslow gently took her upper arm.

'Jess, let the president speak.'

'Sorry president. You were saying.'

Putin walked to Jessica until their eyes were level and just a few inches apart. His feet were on the floor, but two feet higher than hers. She would get Onslow to draw it out for her, later.

'You are exquisite, Mrs Taylor.'

'Jess.'

He smiled.

'We think you English girls all have rotten teeth.'

'You are probably thinking of Coventry.'

'And plump, ruddy faces.'

'Newcastle, mostly.'

'But your skin is olive, your eyes clear. Asian?'

'Me? An agent? God no! I sell dildos, that is all!'

Onslow touched her back.

'Yes president. Mrs Taylor is quarter Asian. Afghan on her father's side.'

'Afghan? My country fought the Afghans and, to be honest Jess, we lost.'

'So did we Mr President. And we also lost.'

'But we have won every other war, Jess.'

Rebel snorted a laugh and coughed into her glass *'Crimea 1856!'*

The president studied Rebel for a moment, before turning his attention back to Jessica.

'I will have my, friends, try out the dildos tonight, Jess.'

'Ah no! Vlad darling, that will ruin my surprise.'

She extended her arm to walk her fingers up his naked chest; she accidentally started on his thigh. The perspectives were wrong, but she was on his chest in two *steps;* she pouted and spoke again.

'It has been such fun meeting you, daddy. May I call you daddy?' She continued to pout.

'Well, Stalin was *Uncle Joe*. So, I suppose so. Although it is a bit creepy.'

'You see Flad…'

'Flad?'

'You try say Vlad with a pout! It is just I have had the dildos programmed to sing you a surprise song for Victory Parade Day.'

'Oh, my sweet!'

'Please call me Jess.'

'I look forward to your sweet surprise, sweet. Then, after the parade we can meet, sweet, tout suite, and we can talk about your surprise. If it is sweet, sweet, I may have to tickle you. If it is naughty, I may have to spank you, sweetly, sweetheart.'

'And I might have to break your fucking arm.'

'Jess?'

'Vlad, daddy. Let me take the dildos to the girls myself. Walk them through the controls.'

'Of course, sweet.'

Putin walked the group to the door – shrinking in stature as they progressed until he barely reached the height of Jessica's knee.

'Sweetheart, my people picked-up on a term referenced on the import paperwork. What does 'micro' mean in English?'

'Micro?' Jessica blushed. She looked to Onslow. 'What is the technical definition of 'micro', please, Onslow?'

''Micro', Mrs Taylor? Um, well, it means really, really, not all that small, Mr President.'

Jessica picked up Putin from under his arms to kiss his cheeks goodbye. He kissed her fully on the lips and Jessica felt pleasantly surprised by how good it felt. Onslow cleared his throat and Jessica tickled Putin to stop the kiss. He laughed hysterically, like the Pillsbury doughboy.

Chapter Nine

The four were escorted through various sanctums, both inner and outer, halls, passages, and porches. Jessica gave the pickled Piper a piggyback, as she lightly snored – pickled into a stupor. Eventually they found themselves delivered to their lavish room.

'Mrs Taylor,' offered a heavily armed butler wearing a lavish suit. 'We were expecting only you. I hope this accommodation is suitable for you all to share. His supreme excellency, the Prince of Russia, has instructed his inner sanctum assistant to take you to the harem, presently. A fork-truck has taken your box of, *delights*, to the harem, with strict instructions not to be opened. Until then, please relax, freshen up, and ring the bell if you require anything.'

The three gazed around the huge, lavish room, containing a huge, lavish, fourposter bed. The butler locked the sturdy lavish door from outside.

'As I am the manager, I should sleep in the middle. Ons, me, Rebel, Peter.'

Jessica pointed to the row of pillows, for emphasis.

'As he is my boyfriend, we will sleep Onie, me, Jessica, Peter.'

There followed a not especially awkward silence.

'Ok. Rebel, Ons, me, Peter.'

'Ok. Onie, me, Peter, Jessica.'

'I think…'

'Listen Goldilocks! …'

Jessica raised her hands in defeat.

'Ok Rebel. I'm easy. Goodness me – you didn't have to come along at all!'

'Sorry Jess. It is just I'm thinking we should go exclusive.'

'NO! PLEASE!'

Jessica fell to her knees wailing. Her three companions looked around the lavish room, awkwardly, in silence, as Jessica wailed. Onslow spoke, awkwardly.

'Anyway Jess, what is the plan?'

'Oh yes. Sorry. I got a bit emotional there. I'm tired. Now Putin is Prince of Russia, does that mean Russia is now a kingdom?'

Peter sat on the edge of the lavish bed.

'I know, I know!' She raised a hand. 'I did two terms of GCSE Geography! No, a king rules over a kingdom.'

'So, what does a prince rule?'

Peter raised her hand again.

'A principality.'

'Does that mean Russia is a principality?'

Onslow spoke.

'I don't think Putin's self-coronation is recognised, Jess.'

'Not recognised by the United Nations?'

'Not recognised by anyone, not least of all Russia. So, I think Russia is still just a country.'

'If a kingdom is governed by a king, and a principality is governed by a prince, does that mean this country is governed by a c…'

There came a knock on the door, interrupting the group. The door opened to reveal an orangutang in a lavish suit. He escorted the group through bomb proof concrete doors to a corridor and a garage containing superbikes, supercars, and super light-arms.

'Super!'

Rebel moved between the items, stroking leather seats, feeling the weight of light-machine guns and sprawling *supermodel-like* over the bonnet of a supercar. She smelt the leather and polish of a white leather superbike seat, just as the inner sanctum assistant arrived.

'Very sorry, but Clyde shouldn't have brought you here. He is new and, at the end of the day, just an orangutan. Right Clyde?'

Clyde extended his right arm as if signalling a right turn, smashing the spotlight on the front of a highly polished, Twisted edition Land Rover. The inner sanctum assistant sighed.

'That leather seat is from Sperm Whale foreskin, miss.'

'Oh, my word!'

Rebel threw a leg over the superbike seat, enjoying the sensation of the cool, slightly ribbed, foreskin surface. She tried, unsuccessfully, to resist squirming against the leather, noting the more she squirmed, the more the leather tightened, and the wrinkles smoothed. She slipped a super hunting-knife from a sheath built into the seat and secreted it into her belt, for later.

'This way, please.'

The inner sanctum assistant led the group, with Peter holding the orangutan's hand, a few doors along the corridor. Outside stood two eunuchs, carrying machine pistols.

'Mr Dalliance, we must stay outside the harem. Ladies, if you go with the guardians, please.'

Onslow moved to object, but Jessica silenced him.

'We will be fine Ons. We only need to prime the girls.'

Inside, Jessica, Rebel, and Peter found two-dozen beautiful women, busy with various activities. Two were using a gym tucked into one corner of the vast reception room, others were on computers, listening to music, studying military plans, or watching television. A couple napped, spooning on a day lounger. A woman in her mid-fifties approached the group.

'Hello ladies.'

Her voice soft, but confident.

'Hey. We are from U-Crane Dildos.'

Jessica extended her arm, to shake hands. The woman returned the gesture. They were still some distance apart and so walked towards each other; arms extended like Daleks.

'EXTERMINATE!' Quipped the woman in a Dalek impersonation, before quickly instructing the guardians to lower their guns as she was only playing – but not before a couple of shots fired in Jessica's direction. 'Of course. We have been expecting you. This is a big day for us.'

'Big? I wouldn't say…,' started Rebel. Jessica interrupted.

'… Yes. From what we hear, you are a deserving group.'

The woman scoffed.

'You can say that again. Miss…?'

'From what we hear, you are a deserving group. My name is Jessica Taylor. Please call me Jess.'

'Jess? Not the famous Jess who shot down one of our jets in Syria?'

Jessica blushed deep red, breaking eye contact.

'No, I know absolutely nothing about the top-secret NATO project *NAPP*, and certainly nothing about the clandestine rogue American *Bridge* system. And technically speaking, the jet was actually in Turkish airspace. But I don't know that either.'

Her two friends and the woman stared at Jessica, in an awkward silence. Peter was becoming an expert in Jessica's awkward silences. She cleared her throat and spoke before Jessica could reveal any more secrets, which she did not know.

'Jess is a common name. My name is also Jess, and I am really common. Mrs Taylor and I have never shot down anything. I used to pick pecks of pickled peppers, once.' The stares moved to Peter. She continued. 'And your name, miss? For my minutes.'

'My name is Anastasia. Please, let us press on. We have a country to run. I mean a harem to run.'

Anastasia guided the group of women and an orangutan to the crate of Rasputin dildos sat on the floor at the end of a long conference table. As they approached, a harlot of young concubines studied their lap tops. They wore ballet tutus, with fishnet stockings and suspender belts, which extended way below the skirt, and knee-high leather boots. Jessica spoke to the group.

'I love your lap tops. May I have a closer look, please?'

The girls nodded and giggled. Jessica stared closer at the top of their laps.

'Wow, the top of your laps are gorgeous! I love your thigh separation.' The girls giggled again. 'Do you enjoy your work? We have met Vlad; he is such a cheeky chappie and a great kisser.'

The concubines all yawned together and made *little winkie* signs with their little pinkies.

Peter stood on tippy toes to peep over Jessica's shoulder at the girls.

'I always assumed concubines are covered in little pricks, you know, like hedgehogs.' Peter assumed.

In an unassuming voice, Anastasia unassumed Peter.

'That is a common misconception, especially among stupid people. But they have certainly been covered in one little prick recently. The Three Little Piggies, as we call them, are Vlad's current favourites, and they are hogging him. Apparently, they huff, and puff at exactly the right moment, and are excellent at blowing. They even hogtie him. But please continue, Mrs Taylor. These Three Little Piggies need to get to market. It is their turn to fetch the groceries for the week.'

The Three Little Piggies nodded and squealed in delight. Jessica took one canned dildo from the box and gently twisted off the top. Perspiration ran down her neck, aware that the activated depleted uranium was unstable and, if overstimulated, could go-off, explode, in her hand. She remembered that first moment she stepped into the shadow of an alley, with Onslow, on the way back to their digs, clutching him firmly. She smiled to herself.

She handed the dildo to the first little piggie. The dildo burst into a rousing rendition of The Red Flag. As the Three Little Piggies sang along, the tip of the dildo gently glowed a dull, menacing, nuclear, deep scarlet.

'The dildo can tell when you are on your period.'

Rest of the harem gathered and passed the dildo around. As each of the women took hold, the dildo restarted the rendition of The Red Flag. Peter made a note in her minutes to check they had paid Billy Bragg's royalties. Jessica continued.

'They all automatically synchronise…'

'That is quite common with women living and working together,' offered Anastasia.

'… so, if you can take them all out of their cans at exactly 12:00 noon tomorrow, please, they will all sing Happy Victory Parade together in high-fidelity surround-sound. Make sure you set them to *extra dirty* for full volume. Then, afterwards, they are yours to use as you wish. A present from us to you.'

'There is no such thing as a free lunch, Mrs Taylor.'

Anastasia wore a serious expression on her beautiful face. Her voice low and suspicious.

'No such thing as a free lunch?' Repeated Jessica, shrugging. 'To be honest,' Jessica offered vaguely, in a fragmented sentence, blushing, turning her face to the left, touching her cheek, avoiding specifics, playing with her hair, and pressing her fingers awkwardly to her lips, 'we hope these free dildos will open the door and allow us to penetrate the Russian market, deeply.'

'You are a terrible liar Mrs Taylor.'

'I am a terrible liar?' she repeated. 'I am not! I am good! At lying! I am!' exclaimed Jessica shrugging, vaguely, in a fragmented sentence, blushing, turning her face to the left, touching her cheek, avoiding specifics, playing with her hair, and pressing her fingers awkwardly to her lips.

'All I am saying, Mrs Taylor, is take your charge card to the canteen, they have no such thing as a free lunch.'

'I knew that!' lied Jessica.

The Three Little Piggies now argued over whom should have first dibs of the dildo. The piggie in the middle whispered a question, which Anastasia repeated to the room, and directed at Jessica.

'Why are they so heavy, Mrs Taylor?'

'They are... of modest proportions.'

'Tiny, you mean Mrs Taylor. You may speak freely, in here.'

'And so, we gave them a little extra mass, to make them more palatable. The weight is critical to the experience.'

On hearing *palatable*, the Little Piggie slid it into her mouth and nodded gleefully to the others; politely avoiding speaking with her mouth slightly full.

'Critical mass, Mrs Taylor?'

Avoiding Anastasia's observation, Jessica reached for the dildo, just as it disappeared up a tutu. She turned the setting to *Daily Go Quick*, not wanting to over stimulate the unstable uranium. The room gasped and purred as Jessica held the vibrator erect – the tiny shaft shimmering, and the polished uranium gland slowly spinning. She squeezed the base of the shaft, and the punk band Pussy Riot blasted the song *Straight Outta Vagina*. She slapped the shaft against her palm and Jeremy Clarkson shouted in Russian: *O dirti, dirti Lada!* The women all gasped again, The Three Little Piggies each brought one hand to their breast and one to their bellies, simultaneously.

'And we don't need to sync manually tomorrow?'

'Nope. Just before noon, each take one from a can and turn it on full. At exactly noon, they will automatically do the deed.'

Anastasia took the vibrator from Jessica, deftly turned it off, and popped it back into the foam lined, heavy, lead can. The women sighed together in disappointment and one of The Three Piggies burst into tears, comforted by her two friends. Anastasia led Jessica, by the arm, to the door as the guardians unlocked it, to let out the group.

'Thank you for your time, Anastasia. Please shout if you have any questions. Please do not let the girls play with them until tomorrow. It will mess with the chips.'

'Fish n' chips aren't cheap, Jessica.'

'Fission chips? I don't know. What on earth. You are getting at. Fission chips? What does that even mean? Even!' Jessica squeaked back her answer, vaguely, in fragmented sentences, blushing, turning her face to the left, touching her cheek, avoiding specifics, playing with her hair, and pressing her fingers awkwardly to her lips. Her heart raced. An adrenaline tingle tingled, gathering behind her underwear. She stared into the deep blue eyes of the beautiful woman standing, slightly taller, in front of her.

'At the canteen, Jessica. The fish n' chips are expensive, but delicious.'

'I knew that.' Jessica lied.

'You are a terrible liar, Jessica.'

The woman leant-in to kiss Jessica goodbye, on the cheek. Jessica thrust her tongue down the woman's throat. The two fell into a passionate clench, and onto a map table showing the position of Russian naval surface ships, submarines, and land based intercontinental ballistic missiles. Little models and markers spilt everywhere.

Clyde the orangutan clapped and whooped as the eunuch guardians prised apart the couple.

Onslow met the group outside, in the corridor. Clyde held Peter's hand and guided them back to the lavish bedroom.

'You are a terrible liar, boss.'

'Yes, Peter.'

'Shall I book you onto our *Lying to Client's* course?'

'Yes, Peter.'

'And shall I get you Anastasia's phone number, boss?'

'Yes please, Peter. I think that is best.'

Chapter Ten

The four lay in bed. Peter lightly snored. Jessica stared up at the ceiling, wide awake. She got her own way – Onslow lay next to her on his stomach, presumably asleep. Rebel lay next to Onslow, arm across his back to claim her territory and to detect and deter any encroachment.

The little one said, 'roll over, roll over.' So, they all rolled over and Rebel fell out. There were three in the bed and Rebel said:

'For fuck's sake Peter!'

Rebel walked around and climbed back into bed, and the little one said, 'roll over, roll over.'

'Ignore her Rebel. She's sleep talking. Rebel? Rebel, Rebel, are you awake Rebel, Rebel?'

'Yes, Jessica! Yes, I am awake! What do you want, except for my boyfriend?'

'Don't blame me, it was my husband's idea. Look Rebel, I can't do this.'

'Good! Now leave him alone and go to sleep.'

Jessica removed her hand from down his pyjamas, for now.

'No, it's not that. I could do Onslow anytime, no problems. I just cannot blow up all those innocent people.'

'Why not? They are Russian.'

'Whoa! Easy Rebel! Where did that come from?'

'You have no idea, Jessica. You have no idea what it is like to have the Russians take over your country, confiscate your farm, lock-up your brothers and send you and your sisters fleeing to the far-flung corners of Europe for safety! You have no idea of the pain and torment.'

'I am so sorry Rebel. Do you know if your parents are safe? I did not know you had suffered such trauma.'

'Mum and dad are fine thanks. They run a chandelier and balaclava emporium called *The Light Brigade* in Briton Ferry, South Wales. None of that happened to me, I am just saying. Anyway, Onie wants Zelenskyy's babies and Peter called you a fascist – so don't just shout at me.'

'Oh Rebel. South Wales. That must be awful. I am so sorry. And, not that it matters, but they are not all Russian. The Three Little Piggies are English, for instance.'

'Are you sure? They were speaking a strange language.'

'They are from Newcastle, like Cheryl Cole. I couldn't understand a word, either.'

'Twerker Cheryl *Tweedy* Cole is English? Well, I never.'

'And I have a bit of a girl crush on Anastasia.'

'You have a crush on anything with a pulse!'

Jessica removed her hand from inside Onslow's pyjamas again, for now and then.

'That is so unfair Rebel! I didn't hit on that guy we saw in the palace today! Even though he was so my type, holding everyone's attention, gazing back at me attentively!'

'That wasn't a palace, Jessica. That was Lenin's Mausoleum. I said *with a pulse*!'

Jessica shrugged, sliding her hand silently back into Onslow's pyjama bottoms.

The two women lay in bed, now both staring at the dark ceiling. The only sound was Peter snoring and the slight rustling of Onslow's pyjama bottoms. He groaned in his sleep and snuggled into Jessica. Rebel eventually spoke.

'Ok Jessica. I hear what you are saying. Leave it to me, and …'

Jessica spoke over Rebel.

'Oh, thank goodness Rebel! Goodnight.'

She rolled over to face Onslow and immediately fell into a deep and peaceful sleep. Rebel slowed her breathing; she synchronised with Jessica and Peter. Somewhere, a Rasputin dildo was probably glowing red and blasting out a rendition of The Red Flag.

*

Jessica woke to the rhythmic rocking of the fourposter bed, her nose squashed against Peter's nose. The little one opened one eye and said:

'Roll over, roll over.' So they all rolled over and Onslow slipped out. There were four in the bed and Rebel said:

'We need our own room, love.'

She winked at Onslow, smoothing down his pyjama top, which she now wore; her own nightdress ripped and flung across the room. She winked again. Onslow winked back. She smoothed down Onslow's pyjama bottoms, which she was not wearing.

'Yes, we do.' Onslow stood by the side of the bed wearing just his cosmonaut pyjama bottoms, already smoothed down by Rebel. He winked, and she returned his wink. 'And, um, sorry I let that slip out.' He winked.

'That's ok love.' Rebel winked. 'It slipped out in the heat of the moment. It was actually quite a delightful feeling. I haven't enjoyed anything slipping out like that in a while.

They both winked.

'And although it slipped out by mistake, I guess I still meant it. I do love you.'

They both winked. Jessica spoke.

'Oh, get a room, you two!'

'I just said that…'

Jessica interrupted Rebel

'And enough with all the winkies, already!'

'Sorry Jess, it slipped out.'

Onslow hurriedly adjusted his dress, slipping his winkie back into his PJs.

'Rebel, thank you for owning the collateral damage situation, last night. I feel so much better. I want a successful detonation, maximum devastation, but with minimal innocent deaths. I also want us all out of the way. Agreed?'

'Absolutely Jess. I was thinking…'

'Please don't go-on Rebel. Don't bring me your problems. Jeez!'

Jessica stomped to the ensuite. She turned to the others. Peter sat in bed, yawning, and picking her nose. Onslow stood facing Jessica making a winkie tent in his PJs, Rebel now dripping off his arm, lipstick and toenail varnish smeared, hair tousled. Jessica smiled.

'Rebel Rebel, you've torn your nightdress. Rebel Rebel, your face is a mess. Rebel Rebel, how could they know? Hot tramp, I love you so; sorry I don't mean to be grumpy. Bowie, I think.'

'Yes,' Onslow replied. 'I used it to cut off Rebel's nightie. Rebel pinched it from the super-garage!'

Jessica picked up the Bowie-knife, and the torn nightie.

'Hey, Jessica.' Rebel called over. 'We will be ok, I promise. And we all love you too.'

The women smiled. Jessica winked. Rebel shuddered.

*

The four heard a thudding from outside the lavish bedroom door. Peter recognised the noise of Clyde banging his chest, and so skipped to open the now unlocked door. They embraced and spent a few moments mutual grooming, Clyde seeming to find more fleas on Peter than she did on him. She concentrated on picking his nose. The others concentrated on getting ready.

Clyde took them first to the super-boys-toys garage, before Peter prompted him towards the harem. Rebel slipped unnoticed into the garage. The eunuch guardians knocked on the harem door. They all waited.

'Are the girls coming?' Jessica asked.

'Probably. They seem to like to, first thing, and I always tell the truth, by the way.' Offered one guardian. 'No, he doesn't,' offered the second.

Onslow whispered to Jessica. *'They must be Knights and Knaves guardians. One always lies, one always tells the truth. You can ask only one question of only one guard. If you can work out the riddle of how to ask the question, you will find the answer to your deepest longings.'*

The three friends, one orangutan, and two eunuchs stood in silence, waiting for the harem women to stop coming and start coming, and for Jessica to work out the riddle and her deepest longing. And they waited. And waited. Waited. And waited.

'Oh! I know... No, forget that. Oh! Ah, wait.' Jessica occasionally squeaked. 'I've got it! Oh, no I haven't. Don't tell me! Wait.'

Clyde held Peter's hand and using his spare hand for guidance, deftly urinated into a pot plant. He yawned. Peter gave his other hand a reassuring squeeze.

'Right! Here goes. Guardian one, this question is for you. If I were to ask guardian two this question, what would be his answer: Does he still miss his bollocks?'

Before guardian one could answer, Onslow interjected with a squeal.

'Is that it, Jess? We are in the middle of a clandestine operation to free the free world from this axis of evil, and bring lasting world peace, we might all die trying, and all you can think to ask is, if a eunuch misses his bollocks! That is bollocks!'

'Please don't shout at me Onslow. You put me on the spot.'

As the harem door opened, guardian one glanced at his colleague. 'What are bollocks?' They both shrugged to each other.

The women all gathered around the group - chatting, kissing cheeks and hugging. One of The Three Little Piggies produced a peeled banana from her skirt, despite having no pockets, and gave it to Clyde. They all carried a lead can containing a reactivated uranium micro-dildo. Once removed from the protective containers, the nuclear material would form a critical mass in close proximity and once vigorously stimulated, form a dirty, dirty, nuclear bomb. The blast would takeout half the military hardware in the Moscow Victory Day Parade, most of the Kremlin and Red Square, and the country's political elite. Jessica had a terrible feeling Rebel had legged it.

The guardians swung open two huge concrete bomb-doors, opening onto an enclosed courtyard. The group followed a painted red path to stone steps.

'Um, where are you taking us, exactly, please?'

The guardians remained silent.

'You used your only question, Jess. Remember?'

'Bollocks.'

'Yeah, that's the one.' Onslow confirmed.

Anastasia spoke.

'We are going to review the might of the Russian military. You are honoured to have been invited to stand with past Russian leaders, dignitaries, politicians, and the great Ras Putin himself, concubines, and women of the harem, as the mighty Russian military parades the greatest war machines on the planet!'

The group remained silent until Peter spoke.

'To be honest, Miss Anastasia – I don't really like guns. But thank you for the invite.'

'And we have a plane to catch,' added Jessica. 'But please pass on our sincerest thank you to Vlad. Have a delightful party and everything.'

Anastasia's neck tightened. Her canned micro-dildo played canned music and glowed red, to itself.

'This is a three-line whip, Mrs Taylor. You will attend.'

The Three Little Piggies giggled. One produced a pink fluffy whip from her skirt and playfully fluffed it at Jessica, three times. Jessica wondered if it was the same Miss Piggie who had produced the banana, for Clyde.

Outside the doors to the famous balcony, overlooking the impressive obelisk Monument to Victory, stood heavily armed Kremlin Regiment soldiers. They opened the doors for the party.

Below, in Red Square, streams of scouts, guides and cadets marched past. Putin was yet to arrive, the salute taken by clapping past leaders including Trotsky, still with an ice-pick sticking from his head, Stalin, smoking an unlit cigar, Brezhnev, Khrushchev, a grinning Boris Yeltsin, and most spritely of all, a barely cold Mikhail Gorbachev with healthy rosy cheeks and angry facial birthmark. Putin had had the birthmark re-sculptured into the shape of the Russian map, for Mikhail's first birthday, after he had died.

Brooms stuck down the back of their coats held the corpses upright. Puppeteers clapped the hands from behind. Other politicians and oligarchs milled around, waiting for the main man to arrive, for the main part of the parade.

One half of the balcony was built like a fairground Alice Through the Looking Glass house, to make Putin look taller than all the guests, again. Jessica bumped her head on the ceiling, again.

The tiny set of rear balcony doors, set into the enormous set of rear balcony doors, flung open to allow a tiny topless Putin to ride in on his tiny thoroughbred horse, again. In Red Square, the invited crowds erupted into cheers. The puppeteers clapped the corpses into a frenzy. Konstantin Chernenko's head fell off. The harem gathered around Putin, covering him in kisses and hugs.

Putin held his stumpy arms out to Jessica. She popped him on her hip and walked to the balcony edge, to watch a column of cardboard tanks, attached to Lada Nivas, drive past. Giggling, Putin stage whispered to Jessica above the noise of the crowd.

'All our tanks have gone. Zelenskyy has thrown them into the Black Sea. Don't tell anyone.'

The couple snogged for two minutes. He was the best kisser Jessica had ever known. He flapped his arms like a hummingbird until she placed him on his box.

'My favourite part!' Shouted Putin, as a line of intercontinental ballistic missiles came into view. 'After the fireworks, I am letting them all off, to fly free to the west! But you will be ok, Jessica Taylor, you can join my harem!'

She forced a thin smile; being nuked now seemed the better option.

Chapter Eleven

Ras Putin jumped and flapped his arms as the parade of missiles came closer. Jessica noted a glimmer of excitement in his jodhpurs, as a feeling of dread caused goose pimples to cover her body – she could not face a single minute in his harem, which was apparently about as long as it took.

The women and girls from the harem needed no prompting from Jessica. With a barely audible 'Ok girls,' from Anastasia, the women all removed their micro-dildos from the lead cans and set them to full throttle. The reactivated depleted uranium vibrators glowed a menacing red and blasted out The Red Flag. They heard Jeremy Clarkson shouting *You are in the wrong gear; dressed as slutty mutton!*

The dildos bucked and gyrated from the women's hands and spun across the floor, forming an ever more compact mass of throbbing uranium. Anastasia ran to the enormous doors, pushing the usherette out of the way and sending ice-creams spinning across the balcony. She pulled at the heavy bolt, but the doors remained locked from the outside. She screamed to the guards outside, but her voice was lost to the crowd and singing vibrators.

Clyde moved to the balcony edge, to stand between the eunuchs who were watching Anastasia's increasingly manic clawing at the heavy doors. She now sat on the floor kicking at Putin's *ras-flap*. Peter, Jessica and Onslow hugged in a group.

'Hey guys. I am sorry. I did not mean it to end like this. But overall,' she signalled to Putin jumping and flapping from over her shoulder, 'we may have saved the free world, the entire world, from nuclear annihilation. But you can't win them all, and we all die one day.'

'Shall I minute that, boss? Look, I don't think Clyde will enjoy being blown up. If ok with you guys, I will just hold his hand until, you know.' She walked off to hug the orangutan.

'So, Ons, fancy that second-night stand?'

'You're the boss Mrs T, and I won't have to worry about Mr T catching up with me, at least not in this life.'

Kissing him passionately, she pushed Onslow back against the heavy doors, pulled up her dress, and pushed down his trousers. They had barely a moment to lose. The dildos were ready to blow. Jessica remembered the blow setting on her Ballpark U-Crane vibrator. She felt the ground tremble. Her ears filled with noise, and her nose and mouth dried, as Onslow sent shudders through her body. She felt her chest thudding like a machine gun being fired into her; the earth truly moved.

'Bloody hell Onslow! That was awesome!' She panted into his ear.

Onslow gestured with his head to Jessica's left. Halfway through a hole blown into the doors, by an antiaircraft missile, sat Rebel astride a scarlet Chak Motors Molot *Sledgehammer Fireblade* superbike;

sperm whale foreskin seat now fully extended and wrinkle free. Mounted above the headlamp sat a fifty-millimetre automatic cannon and either side of the 1000CC engine mounting blocks sat fixed machineguns facing front and rear. Slung in a line under her left leg was a forward-facing SAM missile launcher, still smoking.

The eunuchs raised their machine pistols and levelled them at Rebel. Onslow broke from Jessica to launch himself as a shield in front of Rebel. Forgetting his trousers were round his ankles, he fell flat on his face – exposing his bare white bottom to the world.

'Clyde! LEFT-RIGHT!' Screamed Peter.

Clyde extended both arms in a signal, punching both eunuchs in the temples, and out cold.

'Um, no hurry folks. When you are ready,' suggested Rebel.

As the harem clambered through the gaping hole and towards the harem bomb-bunker, so Onslow climbed onto the back of the motorbike behind Rebel, on the now extended seat. Jessica squeezed onto the rear mudguard. With hardly any room, Peter wrapped her arms and legs around Jessica's waist. Clyde casually lumbered over, swinging his long legs forward onto the rear foot pegs, holding on with his long toes, and extending his long arms around the three human passengers, clasping the solid chassis with his vice-like grip.

With everyone clamped safely in place by Clyde, Rebel stamped the Molot into first gear, dropped the clutch and jumped the balcony balustrade. Ras Putin jumped up and down on his box, laughing and waving to the group. Jessica made eye contact, smiled, and winked.

Propelled by the air displaced by the dirty, dirty, explosion, the superbike and passengers soared high in the sky, above the crowds of invited sycophants, turning to salt shadows below them, in the wake of a nuclear shimmer. Peter clutched Clyde's arm, reassuringly.

The superbike landed awkwardly, but not in silence, on the roof of a speeding train. It took all of Rebel's skill to keep the bike from crashing as it sped along the roof of the train, eventually coming to a halt on top of the front carriage. Nobody thought to put a foot down, so the superbike eventually toppled over, spilling the live cargo across the roof, just as the train screamed into a tunnel.

*

'Tickets, tickets, please.'

'Can we buy tickets from you, please?'

The ticket inspector looked at the group. Onslow had lost his trousers and borrowed Rebel's knickers to afford some modesty. Jessica sat covered from head to toe in plaster dust. Clyde sat wearing Peter's hat and sunglasses, and his lavish suit with a Pepper Pig blanket around his shoulders, as donated by a little girl sat across the aisle. Peter was pecking pecks of pickled peppers from a pickled pepper pot purchased properly from the pickled pepper proprietor of the dining carriage. Rebel had a single smudge of missile exhaust on the end of her nose.

'There is something wrong here.' The ticket collector gestured to the orangutan.

'Mum loves Pepper Pig.' Jessica made a loopy sign with her finger. What is the last stop, please?'

'Simferopol, Crimea.'

'Perfect. Five adults, one way, please.'

The inspector printed the tickets and processed the visa card payment.

'You people are leaving Moscow at just the wrong moment. The news is reporting the biggest and best pyrotechnic display in the world's history, for Ras Putin's first Victory Day Parade as Prince of Russia. Apparently, the display was equivalent to 15 megatons of TNT and some rockets reached the sun. Our heroic cosmonauts can see the show from space. Goodness, I am so proud to be Russian.'

Jessica glanced at Onslow. Onslow blushed, Rebel rolled her eyes, Peter rolled them back and Clyde found a nit behind Peter's ear.

'I thought I felt the earth move earlier, eh Ons?' Jessica smirked. 'And they planned this show, inspector? Nobody... injured, by this daring event?'

'It was a complete surprise to the population Miss. Ras Putin also used the fireworks to celebrate his surprise announcement of a brand new, all female, government. Ras Putin is such an amazing statesman.

Details are still being announced as we speak. A smart cookie.'

'Oh yes, please! We missed breakfast.'

They all took a smart cookie from the ticket collector, except for Peter who had a pecker full of pickled peppers.

'I guess the harem realised what was happening. Obviously, our cunning disguises as U-Crane and Cry-Mia! agents did not fool them. I thought there was more to Anastasia, a clever woman and really quite beautiful.'

'*Oh, beautiful Anastasia is so clever,*' mocked Rebel in a childish voice. '*Jessica's in love... again. Jessica's got a girlfriend!*'

Peter minuted the exchange.

Chapter Twelve

Jessica lay back against her husband's hip, both panting. Jason cleared his throat. Jessica wiped her lips. Jason ran a hand over Jessica's naked chest. Jessica stretched into a sumptuous feline pose. There followed more panting, heavy breathing, wiping, throat clearing, and a long purr.

'Lovely pussy, Jess.' Jason pointed.

Jessica lifted her back to allow the neighbour's trapped, lovely, kitten to escape, and bolt across the bedroom and down the stairs, pursued by Brian, their dog.

'I think you left Russia just in time to miss the crowds and disruption Jess. The population is euphoric!'

'I tried to watch the news on the flight back from Crimea, but Peter and Clyde were hogging the Wi-Fi to play Candy Crush. What happened?'

'You first, Jess. What was your trip like?'

'A bit boring Jace, to be honest. Lots of sales meetings and schmoozing. Ras Putin is not as you'd imagine. But a good kisser.'

Jason playfully slapped his wife's bottom. They both giggled.'

'You better not have gone any further, you little minx.'

She gave his hand a reassuring squeeze. Feeling reassured and squeezed, he continued.

'And that Onslow of yours better not have touched you! I'm still going to rip his head off for kissing you on the aircraft carrier!'

'On the aircraft carrier? Is that a euphemism? He kissed me on the lips.'

'And did he come through with the second nightstand or was he just teasing?'

Jessica processed her husband's comments and replied carefully. She blushed as realisation dawned.

'Ah, right. So, yes. He came through, and gave me a second-night stand, as you suggested. He is using the second nightstand as a knight stand, but notwithstanding that, he stands by his offer. I will collect it in a day or two; he is stood standing-by, waiting.' Jessica continued to blush. '*Shit*,' she mumbled to herself.

'And the business side of the trip?'

'Yes, fantastic, thank you. I had an email from Doc and Bob Marley to say the new Minister for Motherland Satisfaction has placed the first Ballpark vibrator mass order, for the masses. Also, Peter adopted an orangutan as a replacement pet therapy ape for the deceased camel at U-Crane Dildos. Clyde will also enrol as an apprentice in hospitality, as part of a special scheme for asylum-seeking primates. They hope to open a banana, pickled peppers, and red herring takeaway, together. Peter wants to call it PrimeEates. Now, fill me in on the news, please.'

'Well, Putin surprised the world by making an unexpected decision to appoint a new, all female government. They have already recalled all their troops from abroad, unilaterally destroyed all intercontinental ballistic missiles at the end of the Victory Parade and become a self-declared state of neutrality. They have entered a close economic partnership with Ukraine and relinquished Crimea.'

'And Putin made this proclamation, himself?'

'The new prime minister, Anastasia the Great, read the actual proclamation on his behalf. Ras Putin himself is now a non-political figurehead of state and has retired from public life, with immediate effect. Conspiracy theorists are saying he was killed in an explosion during Victory Parade, but only Donald Trump has given that theory any credence on Twitter. The three new joint ministers for Internal Affairs, announced they have already demolished the old Kremlin, to make way for a new, more family friendly, Peoples' Government Centre. The ministers are from Newcastle, and I couldn't understand a word they were saying. But concentrating on the Russian subtitles, I got the gist.'

'Anastasia the Great, eh? Two legs good, four legs bad.'

'They are a very organised new government – they must have been planning this for some time. Every single old member of parliament resigned to make way for them, although Trump says they were also blown-up. He claims to have been staying as a guest of Ras Putin and only just returned to the USA to start his presidential campaign. And then the strangest thing happened. A stray intercontinental ballistic missile, fired from Russia, blew up Donald, members of The Supreme Court who were celebrating overturning of Roe v Wade, and Trump Towers. Everyone else had fled the building when the *incoming* alarm sounded, but Donald insisted it was a fake alarm and so they were all atomised. To be honest, the world held its breath, but Joe Biden was very good about it, saying that any new government can make one mistake, these things happen, and the Russians mustn't worry themselves. So, that is what you missed when you were away.'

'Goodness. Well, it's good to be home.'

Printed in Great Britain
by Amazon